Sketches And Tales

Illustrative Of Life In The Backwoods Of New Brunswick
Gleaned From Actual Observation And Experience During A
Residence Of Seven Years In That Interesting Colony

Mrs. F. Beavan

Contents

SKETCHES AND TALES

Illustrative Of Life In The Backwoods Of New Brunswick

Gleaned From Actual Observation And Experience During

A Residence Of Seven Years In That Interesting Colony

BY

Mrs. F. Beavan

SKETCHES AND TALES ILLUSTRATIVE OF LIFE IN THE BACKWOODS OF NEW BRUNSWICK, NORTH AMERICA,

Gleaned From Actual Observation And Experience During A Residence Of Seven Years In That Interesting Colony.

BY MRS. F. BEAVAN.

"Son of the Isles! talk not to me,
Of the old world's pride and luxury!
Tho' gilded bower and fancy cot,
Grace not each wild concession lot;
Tho' rude our hut, and coarse our cheer,
The wealth the world can give is here."

1845.

These sketches of the Backwoods of New Brunswick are intended to illustrate the individual and national characteristics of the settlers, as displayed in the living pictures and legendary tales of the country. They have been written during the short intervals allowed from domestic toils, and may, perhaps, have little claim to the attention of the public, save that of throwing a faint light upon the manners and customs of that little-known, though interesting, appendage of the British empire. A long residence in that colony having given me ample means of knowing and of studying them in all their varying hues of light and shade. There, in the free wide solitude of that fair land whose youthful face "seems wearing still the first fresh fragrance of the world," the fadeless traces of character, peculiar to the dwellers of the olden climes, are brought into close contrast with the more original feelings of the "sons of the soil," both white and red, and are there more fully displayed than in the mass of larger communities. Of political, or depth of topographical information, the writer claims no share, and much of deep interest, or moving incident, cannot now be expected in the life of a settler in the woods. The days when the war-whoop of the Indian was yelled above the burning ruins of the white man's dwelling are gone--their memory exists but in the legend of the winter's eve, and the struggle is now with the elements which form the climate; the impulse of "going a-head" giving impetus to people's "getting along"--forcing the woods to bow beneath their sturdy stroke, and fields to shine with ripened grain, where erst the forest shadows fell; or floating down the broad and noble streams the tall and stately pine, taken from the ancient bearded wilderness to bear the might of England's fame to earth and sea's remotest bounds.

New Brunswick is partly settled by French Acadians from the adjoining province of Nova Scotia, but these, generally speaking, form a race by themselves, and mingle little with the others, still retaining the peculiarities of their nation, although long separated from it--they like gaiety and amusement more than work, and consequently are rather poorer than the other inhabitants; but, of course, there are exceptions. In the winter I have often seen them on their way to market, with loads of frozen oysters, packed in barrels, and moss cranberries (rather a chance crop); but they looked happy and comfortable, and went singing merrily to the ringing of their horse bells. The French were the pioneers of the province, and often had to do battle with the Indians, the ancient possessors of the soil: of these last there now remains but a fast-fading remnant--objects more of pity or laughter than of dread. Of the other original settlers, or, as they are particularly termed, "blue noses," they are composed of the refugees and their descendants, being those persons who, at the separation of England from America, preferring the British government, sought her protection and came, another band of pilgrims, and swore fealty to that land from whence their fathers had so indignantly fled--they are certainly a most indescribable genus those blue noses--the traces of descent from the Dutch and French blood of the United States, being mingled with the independent spirit of the American and the staunch firmness of the "Britisher," as they delight to call themselves, showing their claim to it by the most determined hatred of the Yankees, whose language and features they yet retain: yet these differing qualities blend to form a shrewd, intelligent, active, and handsome people--intelligence and strong sense, to a far greater amount than could be found in persons of the same class in England. A trace, albeit a faint one of the Saxon serf, still lingers with the English peasant; but the free breeze of America soon sweeps the shadows from his brow, and his sons all, proudly take their place as men, knowing that by their own conduct and talents they may work their way to fortune, or, at least, "rough hew" it, without dread that the might of custom's icy breath can blight their fate for lack of birth or fortune. This gives a noble feeling to the heart and a higher tone to the character, although a sense of the ridiculous is often attached to this by a native of the old countries, when it is shown forth by the "squire" yoking his oxen, a major selling turkies, and the member for the county cradling buckwheat. Yet all this is productive of good, and opens a path for intellect and genius, and when a colonel and member of the Legislative Council eats ***pancakes and molasses*** in a friendly way with his poorer neighbours, is it not likely (as the Persian fable tells us of the pebble lying near the rose, and thereby imbibing some of its fragrance) that some of the graces and politeness of the higher circles, to which these gentlemen belong both by fortune and education, should be imparted, in some degree, to those with whom they converse. So it undoubtedly does, and the air of refinement, native to the New Brunswicker, is never so strongly visible as when contrasted with the new-caught emigrant. Rudeness and vulgarity in glaring forms one never meets from them; odd and inquisitive ways may be thought impertinent, and require both time and patience to be rightly understood.

The state of morals and religion is fast progressing; these, of course, have all their mainspring from education, for an uneducated people can never be, rightly speaking, either moral or religious. So New Brunswick may have the apology for whispered tales that float about, of corn being reaped and wood being felled on the Sabbath-day, and of sacred rites being dispensed with. She is yet in her infancy, and when one thinks that 'tis but sixty years since they first set foot on the shore, where stood one lonely hut, on the site of the now flourishing city of St. John, we must know that their physical wants were then so many that but little attention could be given to the wants of the mind. But now, thanks to the parental care of Britain, schools and churches are rising fast throughout the country, and learning is received with an avidity that marks the active intellect it has to work upon; besides, all these old stories of failings occurred long before the tide of emigration caused them to be enlightened by the visitation of the inhabitants of the gifted climes of the olden world. Well would it be if all those showed as much desire to avail themselves of their means of improvement, as a New Brunswicker does of those enjoyed by him. Their personal appearance differs much from the English. Cooper says, "the American physiognomy has already its own peculiar cast"--so it has, and can easily be distinguished--in general they are handsomer than the emigrants--darker in complexion, but finer in feature and more graceful in form-- not so strong, and fading sooner. Many of the children are perfectly beautiful, but the cherub beauty changes soon, and the women particularly look old and withered while yet young in years. Infantine beauty seems peculiar to the country, for even the children of emigrants born there are much handsomer than those born at home. Such are some of the traits of the natives--then comes the wide circle of emigrants, each (at least the older ones) retaining the peculiarities of their different countries. Many of them, although better off than they could possibly expect to be at home, yet keep railing at the country, and thirsting after the "flesh-pots of Egypt." The Yorkshireman talks of nothing but the "white cakes and bag puddings" of old England, regardless of the "pumpkin pies and buckwheat pancakes" of New Brunswick; and one old lady from Cornwall (where they say the Devil would not go for fear of being transformed into a pasty) revenges herself on the country by making pies of everything, from apples and mutton down to parsley, and all for the memory of England; while, perhaps, were she there, she might be without a pie. The honest Scotchman is silent upon the subject of "vivers," and wisely talks not of either "crowdy" or barley meal, but tells of the time when he was a sitter in the kirk of the Rev. Peter Poundtext, showing his Christian charity by the most profound contempt as well for the ordinances of the Church of England as for the "dippings" of the Baptists. He attends none of them, for he says "he canna thole it," but when by chance a minister of the kirk comes his way, then you may see him, with well-saved

Sabbath suit, pressing anxiously forward to catch the droppings of the sanctuary: snows or streams offering no obstacle to his zeal. The Irishman, too, is there seen all in his glory--one with a medal on his breast, flinging his shillalagh over his head and shouting for O'Connell, while another is quaffing to the "pious, glorious, and immortal memory of King William," inviting those around him to join together in an Orange Lodge, of which community he certainly shows no favourable specimen; but by degrees these national feelings and asperities become more softened, and the second generation know little of them. The settlement from whence these sketches are drawn, was formed of a motley mixture of all the different nations--Blue Nose, English, Scotch, Irish, Welch, and Dutch.

We had been living for some time at a place called **Long Creek**, on the margin of a broad and rapid stream, which might well have borne the more dignified appellation of river--the land on its borders was the flat, rich "*intervale*," so highly prized, formed by alluvial deposits. There are, I believe, two descriptions of this *intervale*,--one covered with low small bushes, and, therefore, more easily cleared--the other with a gigantic growth of the butternut, the oak, and the elm. This where we lived was of the latter description. A few of the stately monarchs of the forest yet stood upon the emerald plains, spreading their magnificent branches to the sunlight, and telling of the kindly soil that nourished them. Along the fences wild hops festooned themselves in graceful wreaths of wild luxuriance. A few clumps of cranberry bushes had also been permitted to remain, notwithstanding the American's antipathy to trees or bushes is such, that his axe, which he hardly ever stirs without, is continually flying about him; but this berry, one amongst the many indigenous to the country, is a useful addition to the winter store--they grow abundantly, and, after the first frost which ripens them they have a brilliant appearance, hanging like clustering rubies, reminding one of the gem-clad boughs of Aladdin. When gathered, they are hung up in bunches, when they become frozen, keeping good till the spring. They are used for tarts and jellies, the frost neither altering their colour nor flavour. Those places are overflown in the spring; the "freshets" caused by the melting of the snow raising the waters above their ordinary level. I have often sailed over them, and 'twas strange to see each familiar footpath and strawberry bank far down beneath the shining waves. As the creek goes onward to the river the *intervale* disappears, and the banks become grey and steep, crowned with the tall and slender stems of the spruce and cedar. New Brunswick is rich in minerals, and veins of coal and iron abound at this place; but many years must elapse ere mines are worked to any extent. A few are in operation at present; but while the pine waves the wealth of her green plumage to the lumber-man, or the new-cleared ground will yield its virgin crop to the farmer, the earth must keep her deeper treasures. In the spring, this creek presents a busy picture. The rivers of New Brunswick are to her what the railroads are now to other countries: and richly is she blessed with sparkling waters from the diamond flashings of the mountain rill to the still calm beauty of the sheltered lake, the silvery streams, the sweeping river, and the unfrozen width of the winter harbour of her noble bay. True, much can be done on the icy ways of winter, but then the home work must be minded, and market attended. Fire-wood for the year must be ***hauled***; the increasing ***clearings*** call for extended fences, and these also must be drawn from the woods on the snow, so that when the spring opens, the roots and other spare produce are quickly shipped off (boated would be a better expression) into large open boats, called market-boats. Another description, called wood-boats, are used for carrying deals and cord-wood, so called from the stick forming the measure of a cord, which is the mode of selling it in the city for fuel. The deals are floated from the saw mills over the shallows, and piled into the boats. One could sometimes walk across the river on the quantities of wood floating about. The larger pieces of wood or timber are floated singly down the stream nearest to the place whence they are cut. This operation is called stream-driving, and commences as soon as the rapid melting of the snow and ice has so swollen the small streams as to give them power to force and carry the huge pieces of timber, until, at the confluence of the streams, the water becomes wide enough to enable them to form it into rafts, on which raft a hut is built and furnished with the necessaries for subsistence. The gang who have been employed in bringing it so far lay themselves upon it, and allow it to float down the stream, until the breeze wafts them to their destination. These are the scenes of the spring, when all life seems awakening. The tree-buds are bursting their cerements--the waters are dancing in light and song--and the woods, before all still, now echo a few wild notes of melody. The blue wing of the halycon goes dazzlingly past, and tells us his own bright days are come; and the "***whip-poor-will***" brings his lay so close, that the ear is startled with the human sound on the soft damp air. The scene is changed when

Sirius is triumphant, telling us of the tropics, and that we live in rather an inexplicable climate. Beneath his burning influence I have glided down this creek when no sound was heard on earth or air save the ripples of the paddle as it rose or fell at the will of the child-like form which guided the fragile bark. The dwellers on the margin of these fair waters are as much at home upon them as on land, and the children in particular are as amphibious as the musk rats which people its banks, and which scent the air somewhat heavily with what, in a fainter degree, would be thought perfume. One can hardly recall these dog-star days at that later season when the pearly moon and brilliant stars shine down from the deep blue sky on the crusted snows; when fairy crystals are reflecting their cold bright beams on the glistening ice, while the sleigh flies merrily along, "with bell and bridle ringing," on the same path we held in summer with the light canoe; when the breath congeals in a sheet of ice around the face, and the clearness of the atmosphere makes respiration difficult. To tell us that we are in the same latitude with the sunny clime of Boulogne, in France, shows us that America cannot be measured by the European standard. A quarter of the globe lies between us; they go to bed four hours before we do, and are fast asleep while we are wide awake. No one attempts to live in the country districts without a farm. As the place where we lived had but a house and one acre of land, none being vacant in that immediate neighbourhood, and finding firing and pasturage expensive, and furthermore wishing to raise our own potatoes, and, if we liked, live in *peas*, a lot of two hundred acres was purchased in the settlement, styled, "*par excellence*," "the English," (from the first settlers being of that illustrious nation,) a distance of two miles from where we then lived. Our house was a good one. We did not like to leave it. Selling was out of the question: so we e'en resolved to take it with us, wishing, as the Highland robber did of the haystack, that it had legs to walk. A substitute for this was found in the universal resource of New Brunswickers for all their wants, from the cradle to the coffin, "the tree, the bonny greenwood tree," that gives the young life-blood of its sweet sap for sugar--and even when consumed by fire its white ashes yield them soap. I have even seen wooden fire-irons, although they do not go quite so far as their Yankee neighbours, who, letting alone wooden clocks, deal besides in *wooden hams*, nutmegs, and cucumber seeds. Two stout trees were then felled (the meanest would have graced a lordly park), and hewed with the axe into a pair of gigantic sled runners. The house was raised from its foundation and placed on these. Many hands make light work; but, had those hands been all hired labourers, the expense would have been more than the value of the house, but 'twas done by what is called a "frolic." When people have a particular kind of work requiring to be done quickly, and strength to accomplish it, they invite their neighbours to come, and, if necessary, bring with them their horses or oxen. Frolics are used for building log huts, chopping, piling, ploughing, planting, and hoeing. The ladies also have their particular frolics, such as wool-picking, or cutting out and making the home-spun woollen clothes for winter. The entertainment given on such occasions is such as the house people can afford; for the men, roast mutton, pot pie, pumpkin pie, and rum dough nuts; for the ladies, tea, some scandal, and plenty of "***sweet cake***," with stewed apple and custards. There are, at certain seasons, a great many of these frolics, and the people never grow tired of attending them, knowing that the logs on their own fallows will disappear all the quicker for it. The house being now on the runners, thirty yoke of oxen, four abreast, were fastened to an enormous tongue, or pole, made of an entire tree of ash. No one can form any idea, until they have heard it, of the noise made in driving oxen; and, in such an instance as this, of the skill and tact required in starting them, so that they are all made to pull at once. I have often seen the drivers, who are constantly shouting, completely hoarse; and after a day's work so exhausted that they have been unable to raise the voice. Although the cattle are very docile, and understand well what is said to them, yet from the number of turnings and twistings they require to be continually reminded of their duty. Amid, then, all the noise and bustle made by intimating to such a number whether they were to "haw" or "gee," the shoutings of the younger parties assembled, the straining of chains and the creaking of boards, the ponderous pile was set in motion along the smooth white and marble-like snow road, whose breadth it entirely filled up. It was a sight one cannot well forget--to see it move slowly up the hill, as if unwilling to leave the spot it had been raised on, notwithstanding the merry shouts around, and the flag they had decked it with streaming so gaily through the green trees as they bent over it till it reached the site destined for it, where it looked as much at home as if it were too grave and steady a thing to take the step it had done. This was in March--we had been waiting some time for snow, as to move without it would have been a difficult task; for, plentifully as New Brunswick is supplied with that commodity, at some seasons much delay and loss is experienced for want of it--the sleighing cannot be done, and wheel carriages cannot run, the roads are so rough and broken with the frost--the cold is then more intense, and the cellars, (the sole store-houses and receptacles of the chief comforts) without their deep covering of snow, become penetrated by the frost, and their contents much injured, if not totally destroyed--this is a calamity that to be known must be experienced--the potatoes stored here are the chief produce of the farm, at least the part that is most available for selling, for hay should never go off the land, and grain is as yet so little raised that 'tis but the old farmers can do what is called "***bread themselves:***" thus the innovation of the cellars by the ***frost fiend*** is a sad and serious occurrence--of course a deep bank of earth is thrown up round the house, beneath which, and generally its whole length and breadth, is the cellar; but the snow over this is an additional and even necessary defence, and its want is much felt in many other ways--in quantity, however, it generally makes up for its temporary absence by being five and six feet deep in April. About this season the warm sun begins to beam out, and causes the sap to flow in the slumbering trees--this is the season for sugar-making, which, although an excellent thing if it can be managed, is not much attended to, especially in new settlements, and those are generally the best off for a "***sugar-bush***;" but it occurs at that season when the last of the winter work must be done--the snow begins to melt on the roads, and the "saw whet," a small bird of the owl species, makes its appearance, and tells us, as the natives say, that "***the heart of the winter is broken***." All that can be done now must be done to lessen the toils of that season now approaching, from which the settler must not shrink if he hope to prosper. Sugar-making, then, unless the farmer is strong handed, is not profitable. A visit to a sugar-camp is an interesting sight to a stranger--it may, perhaps, be two or three miles through the woods to where a sufficient number of maple trees may be found close enough together to render it eligible for sugar-making. All the different kinds of maple yield a sweet sap, but the "rock maple" is the species particularly used for sugar, and perhaps a thousand of these trees near together constitute what is called a ***sugar-bush***. Here, then, a rude hut, but withal picturesque in its appearance, is erected--it is formed of logs, and covered with broad sheets of birch bark. For the universal use of this bark I think the Indians must have given the example. Many beautiful articles are made by them of it, and to the back settlers it is invaluable. As an inside roofing, it effectually resists the rain--baskets for gathering the innumerable tribe of summer berries, and boxes for packing butter are made of it--calabashes for drinking are formed of it in an instant by the bright forest stream. Many a New Brunswick belle has worn it for a head-dress as the dames of more polished lands do frames of French willow; and it is said the title deeds of many a broad acre in America have been written on no other parchment than its smooth and vellum-like folds. The sugar-maker's bark-covered hut contains his bedding and provisions, consisting of little save the huge round loaf of bread, known as the "shanty loaf"--his beverage, or substitute for tea, is made of the leaves of the winter green, or the hemlock boughs which grow beside him, and his sweetening being handy bye, he wants nothing more. A notch is cut in the tree, from which the sap flows, and beneath it a piece of shingle is inserted for a spout to conduct it into troughs, or bark dishes, placed at the foot of the tree. The cold frosty nights, followed by warm sunny days, making it run freely, clear as water, and slightly sweet--from these troughs, or bark dishes, it is collected in pails, by walking upon the now soft snow, by the aid of snow shoes, and poured into barrels which stand near the boilers, ready to supply them as the syrup boils down. When it reaches the consistence required for sugar, it is poured into moulds of different forms. Visits to these sugar camps are a great amusement of the young people of the neighbourhood in which they are, who make parties for that purpose--the great treat is the candy, made by dashing the boiling syrup on the snow, where it instantly congeals, transparent and crisp, into sheets. At first the blazing fire and boiling cauldron look strange, amid the solemn loneliness of the forest, along whose stately aisles of cathedral-like grandeur the eye may gaze for days, and see no living thing--the ear hear no sound, save it may be the tapping of the woodpecker, or the whispering of the wind as it sighs through the boughs, seeming to mourn with them for the time when the white man knew them not. But these thoughts pass away when the proprietor, with his pale intelligent face, shaded by a flapping sun hat from the glaring snow, presses us hospitably to "take along a junk of candy, a lump of sugar," or a cup of the syrup. He sees nothing picturesque or romantic in the whole affair, and only calculates if it will pay for the time it occupies; at the same time, with the produce of his labours he is extremely "*clever*," this being the term for generous or hospitable, and one is sometimes startled at its application, especially to women; the persons in England, to whom it is applied, are so unlike the clever women of New Brunswick, those dear old creatures, who know not the difference between Milton and Dilworth, and whose very woollen gowns are redolent of all-spice and apples.

Towards the latter part of March and April the breaking up of the ice goes on gradually--some seasons, however, a sudden storm causes the ice and snow to disappear rapidly, but generally a succession of soft warm winds, and days partly sunshine and rain, does it more effectually, and prevents the heavy freshets in the rivers, which are often destructive, overflowing the low banks and carrying away with resistless force whatever buildings may be on them. After the disappearance of the snow, some time must elapse ere the land be in a fit state for sowing, consequently fencing, and such like, is now the farmer's employment, either around the new clearings, or in repairing those which have fallen or been removed during the winter. This, with attending to the stock, which at this season require particular care, gives them sufficient occupation--the sheep, which have long since been wearied of the "durance vile" which bound them to the hay-rick, may now be seen in groups on the little isles of emerald green which appear in the white fields; and the cattle, that for six long weary months have been ruminating in their stalls, or "chewing the cud of sweet and bitter fancy" in the barn yards, now begin to extend their perigrinations towards the woods, browsing with delight on the sweet young buds of the birch tree. At this season it is, for obvious reasons, desirable that the "milky mothers" should not stray far from home--many "a staid brow'd matron" has disappeared in the spring, and, after her summer rambles in the woods, returned in the "fall" with her full-grown calf by her side, but many a good cow has gone and been seen no more, but as a white skeleton gleaming among the green leaves. To prevent these mischances, a bell is fastened on the leader of the herd, the intention of which is to guide where they may be found. This bell is worn all summer, as their pasture is the rich herbage of the forest. It is taken off during the winter, and its first sounds now tell us, although the days are cold, and the snow not yet gone, that brighter times are coming. The clear concerts of the frogs ring loudly out from marsh and lake, and at this season alone is heard the lay of the wood-robin, and the blackbird. The green glossy leaves of the winter green, whose bright scarlet berries look like clusters of coral on the snow, now seem even brighter than they were--the blue violet rises among the sheltered moss by the old tree roots, and the broad-leaved adder tongue gives out its orange and purple blossoms to gladden the brown earth, while the trees are yet all black and barren, save the various species of pine and spruce, which now wear a fringe of softer green. The May flowers of New Brunswick seldom blossom till June, which is rather an Irish thing of them to do, and although the weather has been fine, and recalls to the memory the balmy breath of May, yet I have often seen a pearly wreath of new fallen snow, deck the threshhold on that 'merrie morn'. After the evaporation of the steaming vapour of spring has gone forward, and the farmer has operated in the way of ploughing and sowing, on whatever ready-prepared land he may have for the purpose, the first dry "*spell*" is looked forward to most anxiously to burn off the land which has been chopped during the winter--it is bad policy, however, to depend for the whole crop on this "*spring burn*," as a long continuance of wet weather may prevent it. The new settler, on his first season, has nothing else to depend upon; but the older ones chop the land at intervals during the summer, and clear it off in the autumn, and thus have it ready for the ensuing spring. Burning a chopping, or *fallow*, as it is called, of twelve or fourteen acres in extent, is a grand and even awful sight: rushing in torrents of flame, it rolls with the wind, crackling and roaring through the brushwood, and often extending beyond the limits assigned it, catching the dry stems of ancient trees, the growth of the earlier ages of this continent, which lie in gigantic ruins, half buried in the rising soil, and which will be themes of specula-tion to the geologists of other days--it rushes madly among the standing trees of the woods, wreathing them to their summits in its wild embrace--they stand at night like lofty torches, or a park decked out with festal lamps for some grand gala. After this first burn, a *fallow* presents a blackened scene of desolation and confusion, and requires, indeed, a strong arm and a stout heart to undertake its clearance; the small branches and brush-wood alone have been burnt, but the large logs or trunks lie all blackened but unconsumed. These must all be placed in regular piles or heaps, which are again fired, and burn steadily for a few hours, after which all traces of the noble forest are gone, save the blackened stumps and a few white ashes; it is then ready for planting or sowing, with the assistance of the hoe or harrow.

And now, kind reader, if you have accompanied me thus far, will you have the kindness to suppose us fixed at last in our habitation--whitewashing, painting, and scrubbing done, and all the fuss of moving over--our fallow fenced and filled--the dark green stems of the wheat and oats standing thick and tall--the buck-wheat spreading its broad leaves, and the vines of the pumpkins and cucumbers running along the rich soil, where grows in luxuriance the potatoe, that root, valuable to New Brunswick

> "As the bread-fruit tree
> To the sunny isles of Owhyhee."

Suppose it, then, a bright and balmy day in the sunny ides of June--the earth is now in all the luxuriant pride of her summer beauty; for although the summer is long coming, yet, when it does begin, vegetation is so rapid that a few short days call it forth in all its loveliness; nay, the transition is so quick, that I have observed its workings in an hour's space. In the red sunlight of the morn I have seen the trees with their wintry sprays and brown leaf-buds all closed--when there fell a soft and refreshing shower--again the sunbeams lit the sky, and oh! the glorious change--the maple laughed out with her crimson blossoms and fair green leaves--the beech-tree unfolded her emerald plumes--the fairy stems of the aspen and birch were dancing in light, and the stately ash was enwreathed with her garland of verdant green--the spirit of spring seemed to have waved o'er them the wand of enchantment. On this bright day, of which I now speak, all this mighty change had been accomplished, and earth and air seemed all so delightful, one could hardly imagine that it could be improved by aught added to or taken from it.

I am now just going to walk along the settlement to visit a friend, and if you will accompany me, I shall most willingly be your Asmodeus. A straight and well-worked road runs through the settlement, which is about nine miles in length. This part of the country is particularly hilly, and from where we now stand we have a view of its whole extent. Twenty years ago a blazed track was the only path through the dense forest to where, at its furthest extremity, one adventurous set-tler had dared to raise his *log hut*. The older inhabitants, who lived only on the margin of the rivers, laughed at the idea of clearing those high "*back lands*" where there was neither intervale or rivers, but he heeded them not, and his lonely hut became the nucleus of one of the most flourishing settlements in New Brunswick. The woods have now retreated far back from the road, and at this season the grass and grain are so high that the stumps are all concealed. The scene is very different to the country landscapes of England. There there are square smooth fields enclosed with stone walls, neat white palings, or the hawthorn hedge, scenting the breezes with its balmy "honeysuckle," or sweet wild rose--song-birds filling the air with melody, and stately castles, towering o'er the peasant's lowly home, while far as the eye can reach 'twill rest but on some fair village dome or farm. Here the worm or zigzag fence runs round the irregularly-shaped clearings, in the same rustic garb it wore when a denizen of the forest. The wild flowers here have no perfume, but the raspberries, which grow luxuriantly in the spaces made by the turnings of the fences, have a sweet smell, and there is a breath which tells of the rich strawberry far down among the shadowy grass. The birds during the hot months of summer have no song, but there are numbers of them, and of the brightest plumage. The fairy humming-bird, often in size no larger than a bee, gleams through the air like a flower with wings, and the bald eagle sits majestically on the old grey pines, which stand like lone monuments of the past, the storms and the lightnings having ages ago wreaked their worst upon them, and bereft them of life and limb, yet still they stand, all lofty and unscathed by the axe or the fire which has laid the younger forest low. The dwellings, either the primitive log-hut, the first home of the settler, or the more stately frame-buildings, stand each near the road, on the verge of its own clearing, which reaches back to where the dark woods form a back-ground to the scene. These stretch far and wide over the land, save where appears, amid their density, some lonely settlement or improvement of adventurous emigrant. Those little spots, of how much importance to their owners, yet seem as nothing amid the vast forest. Each dwelling in this country is in itself a theme for study and interest. Here, on one side, is the home of an English settler--amid all the bustle and chopping and burning of a new farm, he has found time to plant a few fruit trees, and has now a flourishing young orchard, and a garden wherein are herbs of "fragrant smell and spicy taste," to give a warm relish to the night's repast. For the cultivation of a garden the natives, unless the more opulent of them, seem to care little; and outside the dwelling of a blue nose there is little to be seen, unless it be a cucumber bed among the chips, or a patch of Indian corn. Again, the Scotch settlers may be known by the taste shown in selecting a garden spot--a gentle declivity, sloping to a silvery stream, by which stand a few household trees that he has permitted to remain--beneath them a seat is placed, and in some cherished spot, watched over with the tenderest care, is an exotic sprig of heath or broom. About the Hibernian's dwelling may be a mixture of all these differing tastes, while perhaps a little of the national ingenuity may be displayed in a broken window, repaired with an old hat, or an approximation towards friendliness between the domestic animals and the inmates. With the interior of these dwellings one is agreeably surprised, they (that is, generally speaking), appear so clean and comfortable. Outside the logs are merely hewed flat, and the interstices filled up with moss and clay, the roof and ends being patched up with boards and bark, or anything to keep out the cold. They certainly look rough enough, but within they are ceiled above and around with smooth shining boards; there are no walls daubed with white-wash, nor floors strewn with vile gritty sand, which last certainly requires all the sanctity of custom to render it endurable, but the walls and floors are as bright and clean as the scrubbing-brush and plenty of soap can make them. This great accessary to cleanliness, **soap**, is made at home in large quantities, the ashes of the wood burnt in the fire-place making the "ley," to which is added the coarser fat and grease of the animals used for home consumption. It costs nothing but the trouble of making, and the art is little. As regards cleanliness, the natives have something almost Jewish in their personal observances of it as well as of their food. The blood of no animal is ever used, but flows to the earth from whence it sprung, and the poorest of them perform their ablutions before eating with oriental exactness; these habits are soon imparted to the emigrants, many of whom, when they first come out, all softly be it said, are by no means so nice.

The large bright fires of the log house prevent all possible ideas of damp; they certainly are most delightful--those magnificent winter fires of New Brunswick--so brilliant, so cheerful, and so warm--the charred coals, like a mass of burning rubies, giving out their heat beneath, while between the huge "***back-log***" and "***fore-stick,***" the bright flames dance merrily up the wide chimney. I have often heard people fancy a wood fire as always snapping and sparkling in your face, or green and smoky, chilling you with its very appearance, but those would soon change their opinion if they saw a pile of yellow birch and rock maple laid right "fore and aft" across the bright fire-dogs, the hearth swept up, and the chips beneath fanned with the broom, they would then see the union of light and heat in perfection. In one way it is preferable to coals, that is, while making on the fire you might if you chose wear white kid gloves without danger of soiling them. Another comfort to the settler in the back woods is, that every stick you burn makes one less on the land. Stoves, both for cooking and warming the houses, have long been used in the United States, and are gradually coming into common use in New Brunswick. In the cities they are generally used, where fuel is expensive, as they require less fuel, and give more heat than open "fire-places;" but the older inhabitants can hardly be reconciled to them; they prefer the rude old hearth stone, with its bright light, to the dark stove. I remember once spending the evening at a house where the younger part of the family, to be fashionable, had got a new stove placed in the fire-place of " *'tother room*," which means, what in Scotland is termed "*ben*" the house, and in England "the *parlour*." This was the first evening of its being put in operation. I observed the old gentleman (a first-rate specimen of a blue nose) looked very uncomfortable and fidgetty. For a time he sat twirling his thumbs in silence, when suddenly a thought seemed to strike him: he left the room, and shortly after the draught-hole of the stove grew dark, and a cloud of smoke burst forth from it. The old gentleman came in, declaring he was almost suffocated, and that it was "all owing to *that nasty ugly Yankee critter*," the stove. He instantly had it taken down, and was soon gazing most comfortably on a glorious pile of burning wood, laid on by himself, with the most scientific regard to the laws of *levity, concavity*, and *contiguity* requisite in fire-making; and by the twinkle of his eye I knew that he was enjoying the ruse he had employed to get rid of the stove, for he had quietly stopped the flue. For the mere convenience of the thing, I think a stove is decidedly preferable. In this country, where people are generally their own cooks as well as everything else, they learn to know how the most and the best work can be done with the least time and trouble. With the stove there is not that roasting of the face and hands, nor confused jumble of pots and pans, inseparable from a kitchen fire; but upon the neat little polished thing, upon which there is nothing to be seen but a few bright covers, you can have the constituents of a New Brunswick breakfast, "*cod-fish and taters*," for twice laid, fried ham, hot rolls, and pancakes, all prepared while the tea kettle is boiling, and experience whilst arranging them no more heat than on a winter morning, is quite agreeable. In the furniture of these back-wood dwellings there is nothing rich or costly, yet there is such an air of neatness diffused over it, and effect brought out, that they always recalled to me the painted cottage scenes of a theatre. But here is a house at which I have a call to make, and which will illustrate the "*menage*" of a New Brunswicker. Remember, this is not one of the old settlers, who have overcome all the toil and inconvenience of clearing and building, and are now enjoying the comforts they have earned, but it is the log-house of a new farm, around which the stumps yet stand thick and strong, and where the ringing of the axe is yet heard incessantly. In this working country people are, in general, like the famous Mrs. Gilpin, who, though on pleasure bent, had yet a frugal mind, and contrive to make business and amusement go together; and although I had left home with the intention of paying a visit, a little business induces me to pause here, ere I proceed to where I intended; and even here, while arranging this, I shall enjoy myself as much as though I were sackless of thought or interest in anything save amusement. The manufacture of the wool raised on the farm is the most important part of the women's work, and in this the natives particularly excel. As yet I knew not the mysteries of colouring brown with butternut bark, nor the proper proportion of *sweet fern* and indigo to produce green, so that our wool, on its return from the carding mill, had been left with this person--lady, "par courtesie,"--who was a perfect adept in the art, to be spun and wove: and the business on which I now call is to arrange with her as to its different proportions and purposes. What for blankets, for clothing, or for socks and mittens, which all require a different style of manufacture, and are all items of such importance during the winter snows. Melancthon Grey, whose most Christian and protestant appellation was abbreviated into "Lank," was a true-blooded blue nose. His father had a noble farm of rich intervale on the banks of the river Saint John, and was well to do in the world. Lank was his eldest son, yet no heritage was his, save his axe and the arm which swung it. The law of primogeniture exists not in this country, and the youngest son is frequently heir to that land on which the older ones have borne the "heat and burthen of the day," and rendered valuable by their toil, until each chooses his own portion in the world, by taking unto himself a wife and a lot of forest land, and thus another hard-won *homestead* is raised, and sons enough to choose among for heirs. Melancthon Grey had wedded his cousin, a custom common among the "blue noses," and which most likely had its origin in the patriarchal days of the earlier settlers, when the inhabitants were few. Sybel was a sweet pretty girl, deficient, as the Americans all are, in those high-toned feelings which characterise the depth of woman's love in the countries of Europe, yet made, as they generally do, an affectionate wife, and a fond and doating mother. Those two names, Sybel and Melancthon, had a strange sound in the same household, awaking, as they always did in my dreamy fancy, a train of such differing memories. Sybel recalling the days of early Rome, the haughty Tarquin and his mysterious prophetess, while Melancthon brought back the "Reformation," and the best and most pious of its fathers. In the particular of names, the Americans have a decided "penchant" for those of euphonious and peculiar sound- -they are selected from sacred and profane history, ancient and modern. To them, however, there is little of meaning attached by those who give them save the sound. I have known one family reckon among its members a Solon and Solomon, a Hector and Wellington, a Bathsheba and Lucretia; and the two famous Johns, Bunyan and Wesley, have many a name-sake. These, in their full length, are generally saved for holiday terms, and abbreviations are made for every-day use. In these they are ingenious in finding the shortest, and *Theodore*, that sweetest of all names, I have heard curtailed to "*Od*," which seems certainly an odd enough cognomen. Sybel's bridal portion consisted of a cow and some sheep--her father's waggon which brought her home contained some household articles her mother's care had afforded--Melancthon had provided a barrel of pork and one of flour, some tea and molasses, that staple commodity in transatlantic housekeeping. Amongst Sybel's chattels were a bake-pan and tea-kettle, and thus they commenced the world. Melancthon has not yet had time to make a gate at his dwelling, and our only mode of entrance must be either by climbing the "fence" or unshipping the "*bars*," which form one pannel, and which are placed so as to be readily removed for the passage of a carriage, but from us this will require both time and strength, so at the risk of tearing our dress we will e'en take the fence. This is a feat which a novice does most clumsily, but which those who are accustomed to it do most gracefully.

As we approach the dwelling, the housewife's handy-work is displayed in a pole hung with many a skein of snow white yarn, glistening in the sunlight. Four years have passed since Sybel was a bride---her cheek has lost the bloom of girlhood, and has already assumed the hollow form of New Brunswick matrons; her dress is home-spun, of her own manufacture, carded and spun by her own hands, coloured with dye stuffs gathered in the woods, woven in a pretty plaid, and neatly made by herself. This is also the clothing of her husband and children; a bright gingham handkerchief is folded inside her dress, and her rich dark hair is smoothly braided. In this particular the natives display a good taste--young women do not enshroud themselves in a cap the day after their marriage, as if glad to be done with the trouble of dressing their hair; and unless from sickness a cap is never worn by any one the least youthful. The custom commences with the children, for infants never have their heads covered during the day. At first the little bald heads seem unsightly to a stranger, but when the eye gets accustomed, they look much better in their own natural beauty then when decked out in lace and muslin. The plan of keeping the head cool seems to answer well, for New Brunswick may rival any country in the world for a display of lovely infants. Sybel has the delicacy of appearance which the constant in-door occupation of the women gives them, differing much from the coarse, but healthier look of those countries where the females assist in field labours. The "blue nose" considers it "*agin all nature*" for women to work out, and none are ever seen so employed, unless it be the families of emigrants before they are naturalised. A flush of delight crimsons Sybel's pale face as she welcomes me in, for simple and retired as her life is, she yet cherishes in her heart all the fondness for company and visiting inherent to her sex, and loves to enjoy them whenever opportunity permits. No excuse would be listened to,--I must stay dinner--my bonnet is untied, and placed upon the bed--Sybel has churned in the early cool of the morning, and she has now been working over the golden produce of her labours with a wooden ladle in a tray. With this ladle the butter is taken from the churn; the milk beaten out, and formed by it into rolls--nothing else is employed, for moulds or prints are not used as in England. She has just finished, and placed it in her dairy, a little bark-lined recess adjoining the house--and now, on hospitable thoughts intent, she has caught up her pail and is gone for water--in this we are most luxurious in New Brunswick, never keeping any quantity in the house, but using it bright and sparkling as it gushes from the spring. While she is gone, we will take a pencilling of her dwelling. A beautiful specimen of still-life, in the shape of a baby six months old, reposes in its cradle--its eye-lids' long and silky fringes are lightly folded in sleep on its smooth round cheek. Another older one is swinging in the rocking chair, playing with some chips and bark, the only toys of the log house--this single apartment serves the family for parlour, for kitchen, and hall--the cham-

ber above being merely used as a store room, or receptacle for lumber--'tis the state
bed-room as well, and on the large airy-looking couch is displayed a splendid coverlet of home-spun wool, manufactured in a peculiar style, the possessing of which
is the first ambition of a back-wood matron, and for which she will manoeuvre as
much as a city lady would for some ***bijou of a chiffionier***, or centre table--Sybel has
gained her's by saving each year a portion of the wool, until she had enough to accomplish this sure mark of industry, and of ***getting along in the world***; for if they
are not getting along or improving in circumstances their farms will not raise sheep
enough to yield the wool, and if they are not industrious the yarn will not be spun
for this much-prized coverlet, which, despite the local importance attached to it, is
a useful, handsome and valuable article in itself. On a large chest beside the bed are
laid piles of snow white blankets, and around the walls are hung the various woollen garments which form the wardrobe of the family. Bright-hued Indian baskets
stand on top of each other--a pair of beaded moccasins and a reticule of porcupine
quills are hung up for ornament. The pine table and willow-seated chairs are all
made in the "bush," and even into this far back settlement has penetrated the prow-
ess of the renowned "Sam Slick, of Slickville." One of his wooden-made yankee
clocks is here--its case displaying "a most elegant picture" of Cupid, in frilled trowsers and morocco boots, the American prototype of the little god not being allowed
to appear so scantily clad as he is generally represented. A long rifle is hung over the
mantle-piece, and from the beams are suspended heads of Indian corn for seed; by
them, tied in bunches, or in paper bags, is a complete "hortus siccus" of herbs and
roots for medicinal as well as culinary purposes. Bone set and lobelia, sage and sa-
vory, sarsaparilla, and that mysterous bark which the natives say acts with a different effect, according as it is peeled up or down the tree--cat-nip and calamus root
for the baby, with dried marigold leaves, balm of gilead buds, and a hundred others,
for compounding the various receipts they possess, as remedies for every complaint
in the world. Many of these they have learnt from the Indians, whose "ancient
medicine men" are well versed in the healing powers with which the herbs of the
forest and the field are gifted. On a small shelf is laid the library, which consists but
of the bible, a new almanac, and Humbert's Union Harmony, the province manual
of sacred music, of which they are most particularly fond; but the air of the country
is not favourable to song, and their melody always seemed to me "harmony not

understood," Meanwhile, for the last half-hour, Sybel has been busily engaged in cooking, at which the natives are most expeditious and expert. I know not how they would be in other countries, but I know that at home they are first-rate--no other can come up to them in using the materials and implements they are possessed of. By the accustomed sun-mark on the floor, which Sybel prefers to the clock, she sees 'tis now the hungry hour of noon, and blows the horn for Lank to come to dinner. This horn is a conk shell, bored at one end, and its sound is heard at a great distance. At the hours of meal-time it may be heard from house to house, and, ringing through the echoing woods from distant settlements, telling us, amid their loneliness, of happy meetings at the household board; but it comes, too, at times, when its sounds are heralds of trouble and dismay. I have heard it burst upon the ear at the silent hour of midnight, and, starting from sleep, seen the sky all crimsoned with the flames of some far off dwelling, whose inmates thus called for assistance; but long ere that assistance could be given, the fire would have done its worst of destruction, perhaps of death. I have also heard it, when twilight gathered darkly o'er the earth, floating sad and mournfully since sun-set, from some dwelling in the forest's depths, whose locality, but for the sounds, would not be known. Some member of the family has been lost in the woods, and the horn is blown to guide him homewards through the trackless wilderness. How sweet must those sounds be to the benighted wanderer, bearing, as they do, the voice of the heart, and telling of love and affectionate solicitude! But Melancthon has driven his ox-team to the barn, and now, with the baby on his lap, which, like all the blue-noses, he loves to nurse, sits down to table, where we join him. The dinner, as is often the case in the backwoods in summer, is "a regular pick-up one," that is, composed of any thing and every thing. People care little for meat in the hot weather; and, in fact, a new settler generally uses his allowance of beef and pork during the long winter, so that the provision for summer depends principally on fish, with which the country is amply supplied, and the produce of the dairy. The present meal consists of fine trout from the adjoining stream, potatoes white as snow-balls, and, pulverising on the dish, some fried ham, and young French beans, which grow there in the greatest luxuriance, climbing to the top of their lofty poles till they can grow no higher. I have often thought them scions of that illustrious bean-stalk owned by Jack in the fairy tale. We have also a bowl of salad, and home-made vinegar prepared from maple sap, a large hot cake, made with Indian meal, and milk and dried blue-berries, an excellent substitute for currants. Buscuits, of snow white Tenessee flour, raised with cream and sal-a-ratus. This last article, which is used in place of yeast, or eggs, in compounding light cakes, can also be made at home from ley of the wood ashes, but it is mostly bought in town. The quantity of this used is surprising, country "store-keepers" purchasing barrels to supply their customers. A raspberry pie, and a splendid dish of strawberries and cream, with tea (the inseparable beverage of every meal in New Brunswick), forms our repast; and such would it be in ninety-nine houses out of a hundred of the class I am describing. Many of the luxuries, and all the necessaries of life, can be raised at home, by those who are industrious and spirited enough to take advantage of their resources. Melancthon this year expects to **bread himself**, as well as grow enough of hay to winter his stock. Since he commenced farming he purchased what was not raised on the land by the sale of what was cut off it--that is, by selling ash timber and cord-wood he procured what he required. This, however, can only be done where there is water conveyance to market. The indefatigable Melancthon had four miles to "haul" his marketable wood; but, when the roads were bad, he was chopping and clearing at the same time, and when the snow was well beaten down, with his little French horse and light sled he soon drew it to the place from whence the boats are loaded in the spring. Dinner being now finished, and after some conversation, which must of course be of a very local description, although it is brightened with many a quiet touch of wit, of which the natives possess a great original fund, and Melancthon, having finished in the forenoon harrowing in his buck-wheat, has now gone with his axe to hew at a house-frame which he has in preparation, and Sybel and I having settled our affair of warp and woof, it is now time for me to proceed. She with her large Swiss-looking sun-hat, placed lightly on her brow, accompanies me to the "bars," and there, having parted with her, we will now resume our walk. The next lot presents one of those scenes of desolation and decay which will sometimes appear even in this land of improvement. What had once been a large clearing is now grown wild with bushes, the stumps have all sprouted afresh, and the fences fallen to the ground. The house presents that least-respectable of all ruins, a deserted **log-building.** There is no solidity of material nor remains of architectural beauty to make us respect its fate. 'Tis decay in its plainest and most uninteresting aspect. A few flowers have been planted near the house, and even now, where the weeds grow dark and rank, a fair young rose is waving her lovely head. The person who had gone thus far on in the toils of settling was from England, but the love of his native land burned all too bright within his heart. In vain he toiled on those rude fields, and though his own, they seemed not his home. The spirit voices of the land of his childhood called him back- -he obeyed their spell, and just at the time his labours would have been repaid, he left, and, with all the money he could procure, paid his passage to England, where he soon after died in the workhouse of his parish. Yet even there the thought, per- haps, might soothe him, that though he filled a pauper's grave, it was in the soil where his fathers slept. The forsaken lot is still unclaimed, for people prefer the woodlands to those neglected clearings, from which to procure a crop infinitely more trouble and expense would be required than in taking it at once from the for- est. Our way is not now so lonely as it was in the morning. Parties of the male population are frequently passing. One of the settlers has to-day a "barn-raising frolic," and thither they are bound. They present a fair specimen of their class in the forest settlements. The bushwhacker has nothing of the "bog-trotter" in his appear- ance, and his step is firm and free, as though he trod on marble floor. The attire of the younger parties which, although coarse, is perfectly clean and whole, has noth- ing rustic in its arrangement. His kersey trowsers are tightly strapped, and the little low-crowned hat, with a streaming ribbon, is placed most jauntily on his head. His axe is carried over one shoulder and his jacket over the other, which in summer is the common mode of carrying this part of the apparel. Those who have been ***lum- bering*** may easily be known among the others, by sporting a flashy stock or waist- coat, and by being arrayed in "***boughten***" clothes, procured in town at a most ex- pensive rate in lieu of their ***lumber***. Little respect is, however, paid here to the cloth, (that is, broadcloth), for it is a sure sign of bad management, and most likely of debt, for the back settlers to be arrayed in any thing but their own home-made clothing. The grave and serious demeanour of these people is as different from the savage scowl of the discontented peasant, murmuring beneath the burthen of taxa- tion and ill-remunerated toil, as from the free, light-hearted, and careless laughter, both of which characterise the rural groups in the fertile fields of England. New Brunswick is the land of strangers; even the first settlers, the "sons of the soil," as they claim to be, have hardly yet forgot their exile, a trace of which character, be he prosperous as he may, still hovers over the emigrant. Their early home, with its thousand ties of love, cannot be all forgotten. This feeling descends to their children, losing its tone of sadness, but throwing a serious shade over the national character, which, otherwise has nothing gloomy or melancholy in its composition. There is also a kind of "***looking a-head***" expression of countenance natural to the country, which is observed even in the children, who are not the careless frolicsome beings they are in other countries, but are here more truly miniature men and women, looking, as the Yankees express it, as if they had all cut their "***eye-teeth***."

But here we are, for the present, arrived at the bourne of our journey. High on a lofty hill before us stands a large frame building, the place of worship as well as the principal school-house of the settlement. This double purpose it is not, however, destined long to be devoted to, for the building of a church is already in contemplation, and will, no doubt, soon be proceeded with. The beaming sun is shining with dazzling radiance on its white walls, telling, in fervent whispers, that a shelter from the heat will be desirable; so here we will enter, where the shadowy trees, and bright stream glancing through the garden flowers, speak of inhabitants from the olden world. A frame building has been joined to the original log-house, and the dwelling thus made large enough to accommodate the household. Mrs. Gordon, the lady of the mansion, and the friend I have come thus far to see, is one of those persons the brilliance of whose gem-like character has been increased by the hard rubs of the world. She has experienced much of Time's chance and change--experiences and trials which deserve relating at large, and which I shall hereafter give, as they were told me by herself. Traces of the beauty she once possessed are yet pourtrayed on her faded but placid brow, and appear in brighter lines on the fair faces of her daughters. Her husband is from home, and the boys are gone to the frolic, so we will have a quiet evening to ourselves. The arrangement of this dwelling, although similar in feature to Sybel Gray's, is yet, as it were, different in expression; for instance, there is not such a display made of the home-manufactured garments, which it is the pride of her heart to look upon. These, of course, are here in existence, but are placed in another receptacle; and the place they hold along the walls of Sybel's dwelling is here occupied by a book-case, in which rests a store of treasured volumes; our conversation, too, is of a different cast from the original, yet often commonplace, remarks of Melancthon. 'Tis most likely a discussion of the speculative fancies contained in those sweet brighteners of our solitude, the books; or in tracing the same lights and shadows of character described in them, as were occurring in the passages of life around us; or, perhaps, something leads us to talk of him whose portrait hangs on the wall, the peasant bard of Scotland, whose heart-strung harp awakens an answering chord in every breast. The girls--who although born in this country and now busied in its occupations, one in guiding the revolving wheel, and the other in braiding a hat of poplar splints--join us in a manner which tells how well they have been nurtured in the lore of the "mountain heathery land," the birth-place of their parents; and the younger sister Helen's silvery voice breathes a soft strain of Scottish melody.

Meanwhile a pleasant interruption occurs in the post-horn winding loud and clear along the settlement. This is an event of rare occurrence in the back woods, where the want of a regular post communication is much felt, not so much in matters of worldly importance in business--these being generally transacted without the medium of letters--as by those who have loved ones in other lands. Alas! how often has the heart pined with the sickness of hope deferred, in waiting in vain for those long-expected lines, from the distant and the dear, which had been duly sent in all the spirit of affection, but which had been mislaid in their wanderings by land or sea; or the post-masters not being particularly anxious to know where the land of Goshen, the Pembroke, or the Canaan settlements were situated, had returned them to the dead letter office, and thus they never reached the persons for whom they were intended, and who lived on upbraiding those who, believing them to be no longer dwellers of the earth, cherished their memory with fondest love. Taking all these things into consideration, a meeting had been called in our settlement to ascertain if by subscription a sufficient sum could be raised to pay a weekly courier to assert our rights at the nearest post-office. This was entered into with spirit, all feeling sensible of the benefits which it would bring; they who could afford it giving freely of their abundance, and those who could not pay their subscription all in money, giving half a dollar cash, and a bushel or half a bushel of buck wheat or potatoes to the cause; and thus the sum necessary was soon raised--the courier himself subscribing a dollar towards his own salary. The thing had gone on very well--communication with the world seemed to have commenced all at once. Nearly every family took a different newspaper, and these being exchanged with each other, afforded plenty of food for the mind, and prevented it brooding too deeply over the realities of life.

The newspapers in this country, especially those of the United States, are not merely dull records of parliamentary doings, of bill and debate, the rising of corn or falling of wheat, but contain besides reviews and whole copies of the newest and best works of the day, both in science and lighter literature. We dwellers of the forest had no guineas to give for new books, and if we had, unless we freighted ships home on purpose, we could not have procured them. But this was not felt, while for our few yearly dollars the Albion's pearly paper and clear black type brought for society around our hearths the laughter-loving "Lorrequer," the pathos of the portrait painter, or the soul-winning Christopher North, whose every word seems written in letters of gold, incrusted with precious jewels. In the "New World" Froissart gave his chronicles of the olden time, and the mammoth sheets of "Era" and "The Notion" brought us the peerless pages of "Zanoni," or led us away with "Dickens" and "Little Nell," by the green glades and ancient churches of England. Little did we think while we read with delight of this author's princely welcome to the American continent, what would be the result of his visit, he came and passed like the wild Simoom. Soon after his return to England an edict came, forbidding in the British provinces of America publications containing reprints of English works. Of the deeper matters connected with the copyright question I know not, but this I do know, that our long winter nights seemed doubly long and drear, with nothing to read but dark details of horrid murder, or deadly doings of Rebeccaite and Chartist. As yet, however, this time was not come, and each passing week saw us now enlightened with the rays of some new bright gem of genius.

The postman blew his horn as he passed each dwelling for whose inmates he had letters or papers; and for those whose address lay beyond his route, places of depository were appointed in the settlement. Mrs. Gordon's was one of these, from whence they were duly despatched by the first chance to their destinations on the Nashwaak, Waterloo, or Windsor clearings. Although our Mercury would duly have signalised his approach as he passed our own dwelling, I possessed myself of my treasure here--my share of the priceless wealth of that undying intellect which is allowed to pour its brilliant flood, freely and untramelled, to the lowliest homes of the American world. Having glanced along the lines and seen that our first favourites had visited us this week, our tea seemed to bear with it an added fragrance; and this, although the walls around us were of logs, we had in fairy cups of ancient porcelain from the distant land of Scotland. And now the sun's broad disc having vanished behind the lofty pines, and the young moon rising in the blue heavens, tell us our short twilight will soon be gone, and that if we would reach home before the stars look out upon our path, 'tis time we were on our way.

The cow bells are ringing loud and clear as the herd winds slowly homeward, looking most luxuriantly comfortable, and bearing with them the spicy scent of the cedar-woods in which they have been wandering, and which they seem to leave so unwillingly. Philoprogenitiveness, or a deep feeling of motherly affection, being the only thing that does voluntarily induce them to come home. To encourage this desirable feeling the leader of the herd, the lady of the bell, is allowed to suckle her calf every evening. For this happy task she leaves all the delights of her pasture, plodding regularly homeward at the hour of sunset, the rest all meekly following in her train.

The evening is dry and clear, with no trace of rain in the atmosphere, or we would be surrounded with clouds of those **awful critturs**, the musquitoes, which the cattle bring home. These are often a dreadful annoyance, nothing but a thick cloud of smoke dispelling them, and that only for a time. At night they are particularly a nuisance, buzzing and stinging unceasingly through the silent hours, forbidding all thought of sleep till the dawn shows them clinging to the walls and windows, wearied and bloated with their night's amusement. Those who are sufficiently acclimated suffer comparatively little--'tis the rich blood of the stranger that the musquito loves, and emigrants, on the first season, especially in low marshy situations, suffer extremely from their attacks.

Mary Gordon having now gone with her pails to meet her milky charge, while her mother arranges the dairy within, Helen comes to set me on my way. Again we meet the frolickers returning rather earlier than is usual on such occasions; but there was sickness at the dwelling where they had been, which caused them to disperse soon after they had accomplished the "raising." Kindly greetings passed between us; for here, in this little world of ours, we have hardly room for the petty distinctions and pettier strifes of larger communities. We are all well acquainted with each other, and know each other's business and concerns as well as our own.

There is no concealment of affairs. This, however, saves a vast deal of trouble--people are much easier where there is no false appearance to be kept up; and in New Brunswick there is less of "behind the scenes" than in most places. Many a bright eye glances under Helen's shadowy hat: and, see, one gallant axe-man lingers behind the others--he pauses now by the old birch tree--I know he is her lover, and in charity to their young hearts I must allow her to turn, while we proceed onward.

The fire-flies now gleam through the air like living diamonds, and the evening star has opened her golden eye in the rich deep azure of the sky. Our home stands before us, with its white walls thrown in strong relief by the dark woods behind it: and here, on this adjoining lot, lives our neighbour who is ill--he who to-day has had the "barn raising." It would be but friendly to call and enquire for him. The house is one of the best description of log buildings. The ground floor contains two large apartments and a spacious porch, which extends along the front, has the dairy in one end and a workshop in the other, that most useful adjunct to a New Brunswick dwelling, where the settlers are often their own blacksmiths and carpenters, as well as splint pounders and shingle weavers. The walls are raised high enough to make the chamber sufficiently lofty, and the roof is neatly shingled. As we enter, an air of that undefinable English ideality--comfort--seems diffused, as it were, in the atmosphere of the place. There is a look of retirement about the beds, which stand in dim recesses of the inner apartment, with their old but well-cared-for chintz hangings, differing from the free uncurtained openness of the blue nose settler's couch; a publicity of sleeping arrangements being common all over America, and much disliked by persons from the old countries, a bed being a prominent piece of furniture in the sitting and keeping rooms of even those aristocratic personages, the first settlers. The large solid-looking dresser, which extends nearly along one side of the house, differs too from the light shelf of the blue nose, which rests no more crockery than is absolutely necessary. Here there is a wide array of dishes, large and small--old China tea-cups, wisely kept for show,--little funny mugs, curious pitchers, mysterious covered dishes, unearthly salad bowls, and a host of superannuated tea-pots. Above them is ranged a bright copper kettle, a large silvery pewter basin, and glittering brazen candlesticks, all brought from their English home, and borne through toil and danger, like sacred relics, from the shrine of the household gods. The light of the fire is reflected on the polished surface of a venerable oaken bureau, whose unwieldy form has also come o'er the deep sea, being borne along the creeks and rivers of New Brunswick, and dragged through forest paths to its present resting place. In the course of its wanderings by earth and ocean it has become minus a foot, the loss of which is supplied by an unsmoothed block of pine, the two forming not an inapt illustration of their different countries. The polished oaken symbol of England receiving assistance in its hour of need from the rude but hardy pine emblem of New Brunswick. The room is cool and quiet; the young people being outside with a few who have lingered after the frolic. By the open window, around which a hop vine is enwreathed, in memory of the rose-bound casements of England, and through which comes a faint perfume from the balm of gilead trees, sits the invalid, seemingly refreshed with the pleasant things around him. He has been suffering from rheumatic fever caught in the changeful days of the early spring, when the moist air penetrates through nerve and bone, and when persons having the least tendency to rheumatism, or pulmonary complaints, cannot use too much caution. At no other season is New Brunswick unhealthy; for the winter, although cold, is dry and bracing. The hot months are not so much so as to be injurious, and the bland breezes of the fall and Indian summer are the most delightful that can be imagined.

Stephen Morris had come from England, like the generality of New Brunswick settlers, but lightly burthened with worldly gear--but gifted with the unpurchasable treasures of a strong arm and willing spirit, that is, a spirit resolved to do its best, and not be overcome with the difficulties to be encountered in the struggle of subduing the mighty wilderness. While he felled the forest, his wife, accustomed in her own country to assist in all field labours, toiled with him in piling and fencing as well as in planting and reaping. Even their young children learned to know that every twig they lifted off the ground left space for a blade of grass or grain; beginning with this, their assistance soon became valuable, and the labour of their hands in the field soon lightened the burthen of feeding their lips. Slowly and surely had Stephen gone onward, keeping to his farm and minding nothing else, unlike many of the emigrants, who, while professing to be farmers, yet engage in other pursuits, particularly lumbering, which, although the mainspring of the province and source of splendid wealth to many of the inhabitants, has yet been the bane of others. Allured by the visions of speedy riches it promises, they have neglected their farms, and engaged in its glittering speculations with the most ardent hopes, which have far oftener been blighted than realised. A sudden change in trade, or an unexpected storm in the spring, having bereft them of all, and left them overwhelmed in debt, with neglected and ruined lands, with broken constitutions, (for the lumberer's life is most trying to the health,) and often too with broken hearts, and minds all unfitted for the task of renovating their fortune. Their life afterwards is a bitter struggle to get above water; that tyrant monster, their heavy debt, still chaining them downwards, devouring with insatiate greed their whole means, for interest or bond, until it be discharged; a hard matter for them to accomplish--so hard that few do it, and the ruined lumberer sinks, to the grave with its burthen yet upon him. Stephen had kept aloof from this, and now surveyed,

"----With pride beyond a monarch's spoil, His honest arm's own subjugated toil."

A neighbour of his had come out from England at the same time he had done and commenced farming an adjoining lot, but he soon wearied of the slow returns of his land and commenced lumbering. For a time he went on dashingly, the merchants in town supplying him freely with provisions and everything necessary to carry on his timber-making--whilst Stephen worked hard and lived poor, he enjoyed long intervals of ease and fared luxuriantly. But a change came: one spring the water was too low to get his timber down, the next the freshet burst at once and swept away the labour of two seasons, and ere he got another raft to market, the price had fallen so low that it was nearly valueless. He returned dispirited to his home and tried to conceal himself from his creditors, the merchants whom the sale of his timber was to have repaid for the supplies they had advanced; but his neglected fields showed now but a crop of bushes and wild laurel, or an ill-piled clearing, with a scanty crop of buck-wheat; while Stephen Morris looked from his window on fair broad fields from whence the stumps had all disappeared, where the long grass waved rich with clover-flowers between, and many a tract that promised to shine with autumn wreaths of golden grain; leaflets and buds were close and thick on the orchard he had planted, and where erst the wild-bush stood now bloomed the lovely rose. On a green hill before him stood the lofty frame of the building this evening raised, with all its white tracery of beam and rafter, a new but welcome feature in the landscape. A frame barn is the first ambition of the settler's heart;

without one much loss and inconvenience is felt. Hay and grain are not stacked out as in other countries, but are all placed within the shelter of the barn; these containing, as they often do, the whole hay crop, besides the grain and accommodation for the cattle, must, of course, be of large dimensions, and are consequently expensive. With this Stephen had proceeded surely and cautiously as was his wont. In the winter he had hauled logs off his own land to the saw-mill to be made into boards. He cut down with much trouble some of the ancient pines which long stood in the centre of his best field, and from their giant trunks cut well-seasoned blocks, with which he made shingles in the stormy days of winter. Thus by degrees he provided all the materials for enclosing and roofing, and was not obliged, as many are, to let the frame, (which is the easiest part provided, and which they often raise without seeming even to think how they are to be enclosed,) stand for years, like a huge grey skeleton, with timbers all warped and blackened by the weather. Steadily as Stephen had gone on, yet as the completion of his object became nearer he grew impatient of its accomplishment, and determined to have his barn ready for the reception of his hay harvest; and for this purpose he worked on, hewing at the frame in the spring, reckless of the penetrating rain, the chill wind, or the damp earth beneath, and thus, by neglect of the natural laws, he was thrown upon the couch of sickness, where he lay long. This evening, however, he was better, and sat gazing with pleased aspect on the scene, and then I saw his eyes turn from the fair green hill and its new erection to where, in the hollow of a low and marshy spot of land, stood the moss-grown logs and sunken walls of the first shelter he had raised for his cattle--his old log barn, which stood on the worst land of the farm, but when it was raised the woods around were dark and drear, and he knew not the good soil from the bad; yet now he thought how, in this unseemly place, he had stored his crop and toiled for years with unfailing health, where his arm retained its nerve, unstrung neither by summer's heat nor winter's cold, when the voice of his son, a tall stripling, who had managed affairs during his illness, recalled him to the present, which certainly to him I thought might wear no unfavourable aspect. He had literally caused the wilderness to blossom as the rose, and saw rising around him not a degenerate but an improving race, gifted far beyond himself with bright mental endowments, the spontaneous growth of the land they lived in, and which never flourish more fairly than when engrafted on the old English stem; that is, the children of emigrants, or the Anglo-bluenoses, have the chance of uniting the high-aspiring impulses of young America to the more solid principles of the olden world, thus forming a decided improvement in the native race of both countries. But Stephen has too much of human nature in him not to prefer the past, and I saw that the sunbeams of memory rested brightly on the old log barn, obscuring the privations and years of bitter toil and anxiety connected with it, and dimming his eyes to ought else, however better; so that I left him to his meditations, and after a step of sixty rods, the breadth of the lot, I am once more at home, where, as it is now dark, we will close the door and shut out the world, to this old country prejudice has made us attach a small wooden button inside, the only fastening, except the latch, I believe, in the settlement. Bolts and bars being all unused, the business of locksmith is quite at a discount in the back woods, where all idea of a midnight robbery is unknown; and yet, if rumour was true, there were persons not far from us to whom the trade of stealing would not be new. One there was of whom it was said, that for this reason alone was New Brunswick graced with his presence. He had in his own country been taken in a daring act of robbery, and conveyed in the dark of night to be lodged in gaol. The officers were kind-hearted, and, having secured his hands, allowed his wife to accompany him, themselves walking a short distance apart. At first the lady kept up a most animated conversation, apparently upbraiding the culprit for his conduct. He answered her, but by degrees he seemed so overcome by her remarks that he spoke no more, and she had all the discourse to herself. Having arrived at their destination, the officers approached their prisoner, but he was gone, the wife alone remained. The darkness of the night bad favoured his escape while she feigned to be addressing him, and, having thus defeated the law, joined her spouse, and made the best of their way to America, where the workings of the law of kindness were exemplified in his case. His character being there generally unknown, he was treated and trusted as an honest man, and he broke not his faith. The better feelings were called into action; conscientiousness, though long subdued, arose and breathed through his spirit the golden rule of right.

The days in America are never so short in winter as they are in Europe, nor are they so long in summer, and there is always an hour or two of the cool night to be enjoyed ere the hour of rest comes. Our evening lamp is already lighted, and our circle increased by the presence of the school-mistress.

Although in this country the local government has done much towards the advancement of schools, yet much improvement requires to be made--not in their simple internal arrangements, for which there is no regular system, but in the more important article of remuneration. The government allows twenty pounds a year to each school; the proprietors, or those persons who send their children to the school, agreeing to pay the teacher a like sum at least (though in some of the older settled parts of the country from forty to fifty pounds is paid by them); as part payment of this sum providing him with board, &c., &c., and this alone is the evil part of the scheme; this boarding in turn with the proprietors, who keep him a week or a month in proportion to the number of the pupils they send, and to make up their share of the year, for which term he is hired, as his engagement is termed--an expression how derogatory to the dignity of many a learned dominie? From this cause the teacher has no home, no depository for his books, which are lost in wandering from place to place; and if he had them, no chance for study: for the log-house filled with children and wheels is no fit abode for a student. This boarding system operates badly in many ways. The nature of the blue nose is still leavened with that dislike of coercive measures inherited from their former countrymen, the Yankees. It extends to their children, and each little black-eyed urchin, on his wooden bench and dog-eared dilworth in hand, must be treated by his teacher as a free enlightened citizen. But even without this, where is there in any country a schoolmaster daring enough to use a ratan, or birch rod, to that unruly darling from whose mother he knows his evening reception will be sour looks, and tea tinged with sky-blue, but would not rather let the boy make fox-and-geese instead of, ciphering, say his lesson when he pleased, and have cream and short-cake for his portion. Another disagreeable thing is, that fond and anxious as they are for "*larning*," they have not yet enough of it to appreciate the value of education. The schoolmaster is not yet regarded as the mightiest moral agent of the earth; the true vicegerent of the spirit from above, by which alone the soul is truly taught to plume her wings and shape her course for Heaven. And in this country, where operative power is certain wealth, he who can neither wield axe or scythe may be looked on with a slight shade of contempt: but this only arises from constant association with the people; for were the schoolmaster more his own master, and less under their surveillance by having a dwelling of his own, his situation otherwise would be comfortable and lucrative.

The state of school affairs begins to attract much notice from the legislature, and no doubt the present system of school government will soon be improved. A board of education is appointed in each county, whose office it is to examine candidates for the office of parish school teacher, and report to the local governor as to their competency, previous to his conferring the required license. Trustees are also appointed in the several parishes, who manage the other business connected with them, such as regulating their number, placing masters where they are most wanted, and receiving and apportioning the sum appropriated to their support, or encouragement, by the government. Mr. B. held this situation, and frequent were the visits of the lords of the birch to our domicile, either asking redress for fancied wrongs, or to discuss disputed points of school discipline.

The female teachers are situated much the same, save that many of them, preferring a quiet home to gain, pay for their board out of their cash salary, and give up that which they could otherwise claim from the people. This, however, is by no means general, and the present mistress has come to stay her term with us, although having no occasion for the school, yet wishing to hasten the march of intellect through the back woods, we paid towards it, and boarded the teacher, as if we had. Grace Marley, who held this situation now, was a sweet wild-flower from the Emerald Isle, with spirits bright and changeful as the dewy skies of her own loved Erin. Her graceful but fully rounded figure shows none of those anatomical corners described by Captain Hamilton in the appearance of the native American ladies. Her dark eye speaks with wondrous truth the promptings of her heart, and her brown hair lies like folds of satin on her cheek, from which the air of America has not yet drank all the rose light. From her fairy ear of waxen white hangs a golden pendant, the treasured gift of one far distant. Before her, on the table, lies *Chambers' Journal*, which always found its way a welcome visitant to our settlement, soon after the spring fleet had borne it over the Atlantic. She has been reading one of Mrs. Hall's stories, which, good as they are, are yet little admired by the Irish in America. The darker hues which she pourtrays in the picture of their native land have become to them all softened in the distance; and by them is their country cherished there, as being indeed that beautiful ideal "first flower of the earth, and first gem of the sea." A slight indignant flush, raised by what she had been reading, was on her brow as I entered; but this gave place to the heart-crushing look of disappointment I had often seen her wear, as I replied in the negative to her question, if there was a letter for her. From where, or whom she expected this letter I knew not, yet as still week after week passed away and brought her none, the same shade had passed over her face.

And now, reader, as the night wanes apace, and you no doubt are wearied with this day's journey through our settlement, I shall wish to you

"A fair good night, with easy dreams and slumbers light,"

while I, who like most authors am not at all inclined to sleep over my own writing, will sketch what I know of the history of Grace Marley, whose memory forms a sweet episode in my transatlantic experiences.

Grace had been left an orphan and unprovided for in her own country, when a relation, who had been prosperous here, wrote for her to come out. She did come, and at first seemed happy, but 'twas soon evident her heart was not here, and she sighed to return to her native land, where the streams were brighter, and the grass grew greener than elsewhere. Her friends, vexed at her obstinacy in determining so firmly to return, would give her no assistance for this purpose, fancying that she felt but that nostalgic sickness felt by all on their first arrival in America, and that like others she would become reconciled in time. But she was firm in her resolve, and to procure funds wherewithal to return she commenced teaching a school, for which her education had well qualified her. It was not likely that such a girl as Grace would, in this land of marrying and giving in marriage, be without fonder solicitations to induce her to remain, and a tall blue nose, rejoicing in the appellation of Leonidas van Wort, and lord of six hundred noble acres, was heard to declare one fall, that she, for an Irish girl, was "raal downright good-looking," and guessed he knew which way "his tracks would lay when snow came." Snow did come, and Leonidas, arrayed in his best "go-to-meeting style," geared up his sleigh, and what with bear skins and bells, fancying himself and appurtenances enough to charm the heart of any maid or matron in the back woods, set off to spark Grace Marley. "Sparking," the term used in New Brunswick for courtship, now that the old fashion of "bundling" is gone out, occupies much of the attention (as, indeed, where does it not?) of young folks. They, for this purpose, take Moore's plan of lengthening their days, by "stealing a few hours from the night," and generally breathe out their tender vows, not beneath the "milk-white thorn," but by the soft dim light of the birch-wood fire; the older members of the family retiring and leaving the lovers to their own sweet society.

Although it has been sometimes observed that mothers who, in their own young days, have been versed in this custom, insist most pertinaciously in sitting out the wooer, in spite of insinuations as to the pleasure their absence would occasion, still keep their easy chair, with unwearied eyes and fingers busied in their everlasting knitting. Grace's beau was most hospitably received by her aunt and uncle, who considering him quite an "eligible," wished to further him all in their power, soon left the pair to themselves, telling Grace that it would be the height of rudeness not to follow the custom of the country. She politely waited for Leonidas to commence the conversation, but he, unused to her proceeding, could say nothing, not even ask her if she liked maple sugar; and so, being unused to deep study, while thinking how to begin, fell asleep, a consummation Grace was most delighted to witness. By the fire stood the small American churn, which, as is often the case in cold weather, had been placed there to be in readiness for the morrow; this Grace, with something of the quiet humour which made Jeanie Deans treat Dumbie-dykes to fried peats in place of collops, she lifted and placed it by the sleeper's side, throwing over it a white cloth, which fell like folds of drapery, and softly retired to rest herself. Her uncle, on coming into the room at the dawn of morning, beheld the great Leonidas still sleeping, and his arm most lovingly encircling the churn dash, which no doubt in his dreams he mistook for the taper waist of Grace, when the loud laugh of the old man and his "helps," who had now risen, roused him. He got up and looked round him, but, with the Spartan firmness of his name-sake, said nothing, but went right off and married his cousin Prudence Prague, who could do all the sparking talk herself.

Many another lover since then had Grace--many a mathematical schoolmaster, to whom Euclid was no longer a mystery, became, for her sake, puzzled in the problem of love, and earnestly besought her to solve the question he gave, with the simple statement of yes. But still her heart was adamant, and still she was unwon, and sighed more deeply for her island home. She disliked the country, and its customs more. Her religion was Roman catholic, and she cherished all the tenets of her faith with the deepest devotion. I remember calling on her one Sunday morning and finding her alone in her solitary dwelling; her relations, themselves catholics, having gone, and half the settlement with them, to meeting, but she preferred her solitude rather than join in their unconsecrated worship. This want of their own peculiar means of grace is much felt by religiously inclined persons in the forest settlements, and this made her wish more earnestly for the closing of the year to come, when, with the produce of her school labours, she would be enabled to leave.

Such was, up to this period, what I knew of Grace's character and history. I was extremely fond of her society and conversation, as she, coming from that land of which 'tis said, her every word, her wildest thought, is poetry, had, in her imaginings, a twilight tinge of blue, which made her remarks truly delightful. She had become a little more softened in her prejudice, especially as she expected soon to leave the country, so that one day during her stay with us, in this same bright summer weather, I induced her to accompany me to a great baptist meeting, to be held in a river settlement some four or five miles off. On reaching the creek, the rest of our party, who had acquired the true American antipathy to pedestrianism, proceeded in canoes and punts to the place, but we preferred a walk to the dazzling glare of the sunshine on the water, so took not the highway, but a path through the forest, called the blazed track, from a chip or slice being made on the trees to indicate its line, and which you must keep sight of, or else go astray in the leafy labyrinth.

When I first trod the woods of New Brunswick, I fancied wild animals would meet me at each step--every black log was transformed into some shaggy monster--visions of bears and lucifee's were ever before me--but these are now but rarely seen near the settlements, although bruin will sometimes make a descent on the sheepfolds; yet they have generally retreated before the axe, along with the more valuable moose deer and caraboo, with which the country used to abound. The ugliest animal I ever saw was a huge porcupine, which came close to the door and carried off, one by one, a whole flock of young turkies; and the boldest, the beautiful foxes, which are also extremely destructive to the poultry; so that in walking the woods one need not be afraid, even if a bear's foot-print be indented in the soil, as perhaps he is then far enough off, and besides 'tis only in the hungry spring, after his winter's sleep, he is carniverous, preferring in summer the roots, nuts, and berries with which the forest supplies him. The living things one sees are quite harmless--the bright eyed racoon looking down upon us through the branches, or the squirrels hopping from spray to spray, a mink or an otter splashing through the pond of a deserted beaver dam, from which the ancient possessors have also retired, and a hare or sable gliding in the distance, are all the animals one usually sees, with flocks of partridges, so tame that they stir not from you, and there being no game laws, these free denizens of the wild are the property of all who choose to claim them.

The forests, especially in the hard wood districts, are beautiful in their fresh unbroken solitude--not the solitude of desolation, but the young wild loveliness of the untamed earth. The trees stand close and thick, with straight pillar-like stems, unbroken by leaf or bough, which all expand to the summit, as if for breathing space. There is little brush wood, but myriads of plants and creepers, springing with the summer's breath. The beautiful dog-wood's sweeping sprays and broad leaves, the maiden-hairs glossy wreathes and pearly buds, and the soft emerald moss, clothing the old fallen trees with its velvet tapestry, and hiding their decay with its cool rich beauty, while the sun light falls in golden tracery down the birch trees silver trunk, and the sparkling water flashes in the rays, or sings on its sweet melody unseen amid the luxuriant vegetation that conceals it.

Through this sweet path we held on our way, talking of every bard who has said or sung the green wood's glories, whose fancied beauties were here all realized. As we neared the clearings, we met frequent groups of blue nose children gathering, with botanical skill, herbs for dyeing, or carrying sheets of birch bark, which, to be fit for its many uses, must be peeled from the trees in the full moon of June. On these children, beautiful as young Greeks, with lustrous eyes and faultless features, Grace said she could hardly yet look without an instinctive feeling of awe and pity, cherishing as she did the partiality of her creed and nation for infant baptism. To her there was something awful, in sight of those unhallowed creatures, whose brows bore not the first symbol of christianity. We having passed through the woods, were soon in a large assemblage of native and adopted colonists.

The greater number of the native population, I think, are baptists, and their ministers are either raised among themselves, or come from the United States; or Nova Scotia. Once in every year a general association is convened of the members of the society throughout the province, the attendance on which gives ample proof of the greatness of their numbers, as well as their fervency of feeling. This association is held in a different part of the province each season--and generally lasts a week. Reports are here made of the progress of their religion, the state of funds, and of all other matters connected with the society. There is, generally, at these conventions a revival of religious feeling, and during the last days numerous converts are made and received by baptism into the church. This meeting is looked forward too by the colonists with many mingled feelings. By the grave and good it is hailed as an event of sacred importance, and by the gay and thoughtless as a season of sight-seeing and dress-displaying. Those in whose neighbourhood it was last year are glad it is not be so this time; and those near the place it is to be held, are calculating the sheep and poultry, the molasses and flour it will take to supply the numerous guests they expect on the occasion--open tables being kept at taverns, and private houses are so no longer, but hospitably receive all who come. No harvest is reaped by exorbitant charges for lodging, and all that is expected in return, is the same clever treatment when their turn comes. This convocation, occurring in the leisure spell between the end of planting and the commencement of haying, is consequently no hindrance to the agricultural part of the community; and old and young "off they come" from Miramichi, from Acadia, and the Oromocto, in shay and waggon, steam-boat and catamaran, on horseback or on foot, as best they can. This day, one towards the conclusion, the large frame building was crowded to excess, and outside were gathered groups, as may be seen in some countries around the catholic chapels. Within, the long tiers of benches display as fair an array of fashion and flowers as would be seen in any similar congregation in any country. The days of going to meeting in home-spun and raw hide moccasins are vanishing fast all through the province. These are the solid constituents of every-day apparel, but for holidays, even the bush maiden from the far-off settlements of the gulph shore has a lace veil and silken shawl, and these she arranges with infinitely more taste and grace than many a damsel whose eye has never lost sight of the clearings. By far the greater portion of the assembly have the dark eyes and intellectual expression of face which declares them of American origin; and, sprinkled among them, are the features which tell of England's born. The son of Scotland, too, is here, although unwont to grace such gatherings with his presence; yet this is an event of rare importance, and from its occurrence in his immediate neighbourhood, he has come, we dare not say to scoff, and yet about his expressive mouth their lingers a slight curl of something like it. And here, too, the Hibernian forgets his prejudices in the delight of being in a crowd. I do not class my friend Grace along with this common herd, but even she became as deeply interested as others in the discussion which was now going forward--this was the time of transacting business, and the present subject one which had occupied much attention. It was the appropriation of certain funds--whether they should be applied towards increasing their seminary, so as to fit it for the proper education of ministers for their church, or whether they should not be applied to some other purpose, and their priesthood be still allowed to spring uncultured from the mass. The different opinions expressed regarding this, finely developed the progress of mind throughout the land. Some white-headed fathers of the sect, old refugees, who had left the bounds of civilization before they had received any education, yet who had been gifted in the primitive days of the colony to lead souls from sin, sternly declaimed against the education system, declaring that grace, and grace alone, was what formed the teacher. All else was of the earth earthy, and had nought to do with heavenly things. One said that when he commenced preaching he could not read the bible--he could do little more now, and yet throughout the country many a soul owned its sickness to have been healed through him. Another then rose and answered him--a native of the province, and of his own persuasion, but who had drank from the springing fountains of science and of holiness--the bright gushing of whose clear streams sparkled through his discourse. I have since forgotten his language, but I know that at the time nothing I had ever heard or read entranced me as did it, glowing as it was with the new world's fervency of thought, and the old world's wealth of learning. He pleaded, as such should, for extended education, and his mighty words had power, and won the day. The old men, stern in their prejudices as their zeal, were conquered, and the baptists have now well conducted establishments of learning throughout the province.

This discussion occupied the morning, and, at noon, we were invited home to dinner by a person who sat next us at the meeting, but whom we had never before seen. Some twelve or fourteen others formed our party, rather a small one considering, but we were the second relay, another party having already dined and proceeded to the meeting house, where religious worship had commenced as soon as we left. Our meal was not so varied in its details of cookery as the wealthier blue noses love to treat their guests with. The number to be supplied, and the quantity of provisions required, prevented this. It consisted of large joints of veal and mutton, baked and boiled, with a stately pot-pie, on its ponderous platter,--the standing dish in all these parts. Soon after dinner we were given to understand the dipping was about to commence; and walked along the shore to the place appointed for the purpose, in the bright blue waters of the bay, which is here formed by an inlet of the chief river of the province, the silver-rolling St. John. The scene around us was wondrously rich and lovely--the bright green intervale meadows with their lofty trees, the cloudless sky, the flashing waters, and the balmy breeze, which bore the breath of the far-off spruce and cedars. From the assembled throng, who had now left the meeting-house, arose the hymns which form the principal part of their worship.

I have said the New Brunswickers are not, as yet, greatly favoured with the gift of music; this may, in a great measure, arise from deficient cultivation of the science, but at this time there was something strange and pleasant in the quick chaunting strain they raised, so different from the solemn sounds of sacred melody usual in other countries; and even Grace, accustomed to the organ's pealing grandeur and lofty anthems of her own church, was pleased with it. Still singing the minister entered the water, the converts one by one joining him, and singly became encircled in the shining waves: many of them were aged and bowed with time, and now took up the cross in their declining days; and others of the young and fair, who sought their creator in youth. It was wondrous now to think of this once lonely stream of the western world, the Indian's own Ounagandy. A few years since no voice had broke on its solitude save the red man's war-whoop, or his shrieking death song--no form been shadowed on its depths but the wild bird's wing, or the savage speeding on the blood chase. Now its living pictures told the holy records of the blessed east, and its waters typed the healing stream of Jordan. After some more singing and prayers offered for the newly-baptized, the ceremony was finished. 'Tis strange that on these dipping occasions no cold is caught by the converts. I suppose the excitement of the mind sustains the body; but persons are often baptised in winter, in an opening made through the ice for the purpose, and walk with their garments frozen around them without inconvenience, seeming to prove the efficacy of hydropathy, by declaring how happy and comfortable they feel. We, at the conclusion of the prayers, left the place, and proceeded homewards in a canoe; this is a mode of locomotion much liked by the river settlers, but to a stranger anything but agreeable. They glide along the waters swift and smooth, but a slight cause upsets them, and as perhaps you are not exactly certain about being born to be hanged, you must sit perfectly still--you are warned to do this, but if you are the least nervous, you will hardly dare to breathe, much less move, and this, in a journey of any length, is not so pleasant. This feeling, however, custom soon dispels; and when one sees little fairy girls paddling themselves and a cargo of brothers and sisters to school, or women with babies taking their wool to the carding mill, they feel ashamed, and learn to keep the true balance.

Our light skiff, or bark rather, as it might be truely styled, being a veritable Indian canoe, made of birch bark most cunningly put together, these being so light as to float in shallow water, and to be easily removed, are for this reason preferred by the Indians to more solid materials, who carry them on their backs from stream to stream during their peregrinations through the country, soon bore us over the diamond water, whose mirrored surface we scarcely stirred, to the landing place, whose marshy precincts were now all gemmed with the golden and purple flowers of the sweet flag or calamus; and as the sun was yet high in the glorious blue, we resolved to spend the remainder of the day with a family living near; feeling, in this land of New Brunswick, no qualms about a sudden visitation, knowing that a people so proverbial for being "wide awake" can never be taken unawares. Their dwelling, a large frame building painted most gaily in the bright warm hues the old Dutch fancies of the states love to cherish, stands in the centre of rich parks of intervale. The porch is here, as well as at the more humble log-house, answering as it does in summer for a cool verandah, and in winter as a shelter from the snows. This, the taste of the country artist has erected on pillars, not recognisable as belonging to any known order of architecture, yet here esteemed as tasty and beautiful, and, as is his custom in the afternoon, is seated the owner of the dwelling, Silas Mavin, one of that fast declining remnant--the refugees. He had come from the United States at the revolution, and possessed himself of this fair heritage in the days when squatting was in vogue; those palmy days which the older inhabitants love to recall, when government had not to be petitioned, as it has now, for leave to purchase land, and when, in place of the now many-worded grant, with its broad seals and official signatures, people made out their own right of possession by raising their log-house, and placing the sign manual of their axe in whatever trees they chose; when moose and caraboo were plentiful as sheep and oxen are now; when salmon filled each stream, and the wood-sheltered clearings ripened the Indian corn without failing.

In this land, young as it is, there are those who mourn for the times gone by, and consider the increasing settlement of the country as their worst evil; wilfully closing their eyes against improvement, they see not the wide fields, waving fair with grass and wheat, but think it was better when the dense forest shut out the breeze and reflected the sunbeams down with greater strength on the corn, so dearly loved by the American. They hear not the sound of the busy mill when they mourn for the fish-deserted brooks, and forget that when moose meat was more plentiful than now bread stuffs were ground in the wearying hand-mill. One of this respectable class of grumblers was our present acquaintance, and here he sat in his porch, with aspect grave as the stoics--his tall form, although in ruins now, was stately in decay as the old forest's pines. His head was such as a phrenologist would have loved to look upon; the true platonic breadth of brow, and lofty elevation of the scalp silvered over, told of a mind fitting in its magnitude to spring from that gigantic continent whose streams are mighty rivers and whose lakes are seas; but, valueless as these, when embosomed in their native woods, were the treasures of the old man's mind, unawakened as they were by education, and unpolished even by contact with the open world, yet still, amid the crust contracted in the life he had led, rays of the inward diamond glittered forth. The wilderness had always been his dwelling--in the land he had left, his early days had been passed in hunting the red deer or the red man on the Prairie fields--there, with the true spirit of the old American, he had learned to treat the Indian as "varment," although a kindlier feeling was awakened towards them in this country, where white as well as red were recipients of England's bounty, and many a tale of wild pathos or dark horror has he told of the experience of his youth with the people of the wild. In New Brunswick his days had passed more peacefully. He sat this evening with his chair poised in that aerial position on one leg which none but an American can attain. Ambitious emigrants, wishing to be thought cute, attempt this delicate point of Yankee character, but their awkwardness falling short of the easy swing necessary for the purpose, often brings them to the ground. A beautiful English cherry tree, with its snowy wreathes in full blow, stood before him; he had raised it from the seed, and loved to look upon it. It had evidently been the object of his meditations, and served him now as a type wherewith to illustrate his remarks respecting the meeting we had attended--like those professors of religion we to-day heard, he said, was his beautiful cherry tree. It gave forth fair green leaves of promise and bright truth-seeming blossoms, but in summer, when he sought for fruit there was none; and false as it, were they of words so fair and deeds so dark, and he'd "double sooner trust one who laughed more and prayed less, than those same whining preachers." This was the old man's opinion, not only respecting the baptists, but all other sects as well. What his own ideas of religion were I never could make out. Universalism I fancied it was, but differing much from the theories of those evanescent preachers who sometimes flashed like meteors through the land, leaving doubt and recklessness in their path. The first truths of Christianity had been imparted to him, and these, mingling with his own innate ideas of veneration, formed his faith; as original, though more lofty in its aspirations, than the wild Indian's who tells of the flowery land of souls where the good spirit dwells, and where buffalo and deer forsake not the hunting grounds of the blessed. He held no outward form or right of sanctity. The ceremony which bound him to his wife was simply legal, having been read over by the nearest magistrate. His children were unbaptised, and the green graves of his household were in his own field, although a public burying-ground was by the meeting-house of the settlement.

Meanwhile the old lady, who had hailed our advent with the hospitality of her country, set about preparing our entertainment. Tradition says of the puritans, the pilgrims of New England, that when they first stood on Plymouth Rock, on their first arrival from Europe, they bore the bible under one arm and a cookery book under the other. Now, as to their descendants, the refugees, I am not exactly sure if, when they pilgrimised to New Brunswick, they were so careful of the bible, but I am certain they retain the precepts of the cookery book, and love to embody them when they may. Soon as a guest comes within ken of a blue nose, the delightful operations commence. The poorer class shifting with Johnny-cake and pumpkin, while, with the better off, the airy phantoms of custard and curls, which flit through their brains, are called into tangible existence. The air is impregnated with allspice and nutmeg--apple "sarce" and cranberry "persarves" become visible, while sal-a-ratus and molasses are evidently in the ascendant.

And now, while our hostess of this evening busied herself in compounding these sweet mysteries, the old man related to us the following love passage of his earlier days, which I shall give in my own language, although his original expressions rendered it infinitely more interesting.

THE INDIAN BRIDE,
A REFUGEE'S STORY.

On the margin of a bright blue western stream stood a small fort, surrounding the dwellings of some hunters who had penetrated thus far into the vast wilderness to pursue their calling. The huts they raised were rude and lowly, and yet the walls surrounding them were high and lofty. Piles of arms filled their block house, and a constant guard was kept. These precautions were taken to protect them from the Indians, whose ancient hunting grounds they had intruded on, and whose camp was not far distant. Deadly dealings had passed between them, but the whites, strong in number and in arms, heeded little the settled malice of their foes, and after taking the usual precautions of defence, carried on their hunting, shooting an Indian, or ought else that came across them, while the others, savage and unrelenting, kept on their trail in hope of vengeance.

Strange was it, that in an atmosphere dark as this, the light of love should beam. Leemah, a beautiful Indian girl, met in the forest a young white hunter. She loved, and was beloved in return. The roses of the few summers she had lived glowed warm upon her cheek, and truth flashed in the guileless light of her deep dark eyes--but Leemah was already a bride, betrothed in childhood to a chieftain of her tribe; he had now summoned her to his dwelling, and her business in the forest was collecting materials for her bridal store of box and basket. Her sylph-like form of arrowy grace was arrayed in his wedding gifts of costly furs, and glittering bright with bead and shell. But few were the stores that Leemah gathered for her Indian chief. The burning noon was passed with her white love in the leafy shade--there she brought for him summer berries, and gathered for him the water cup flower, with its cooling draught of fragrant dew. Her time of marriage came, and at midnight it was to be celebrated with torch light and dance. The other hunters knew the love of Silas for the gem of the wilderness, and readily offered their assistance in his project of gaining her. To them, carrying off an Indian girl was an affair of light moment, and at dark of night, with their boat and loaded rifles, they proceeded up the stream towards the Indian village. As they drew near, the wild chaunt of the bridal song was heard, and as all silently they approached the shore, the red torch light gleamed out upon the scene of mystic splendour. The chieftains of the tribe in stately silence stood around. The crimson beams lit up the plumes upon their brow, and showed in more awful hues the fearful lines of their painted faces, terrible at the festival as on the field of battle. The squaws, in their gayest garb, with mirrors flashing on their breasts, and beads all shining as they moved, danced round the betrothed; and there she stood, the love-lorn Leemah, her black hair all unbraided, and her dark eyes piercing the far depths of night, as if looking for her lover. Nor looked she long in vain, for suddenly and fearlessly Silas sprung upon the shore, dashed through the circle, and bore off the Indian bride to his bark. Then rose the war-shout of her people, while pealed among them the rifles of the hunters. Again came the war-whoop, mingled with the death shriek of the wounded. A hunter stood up and echoed them in mockery, but an arrow quivered through his brain and he was silent, while the stream grew covered with shadowy canoes, filled with dark forms shouting for revenge. On came they with lightning's speed, and on sped the hunters knowing now that their only safety was in flight. On dashed they through the waters which now began to bear them forward with wondrous haste. A thought of horror struck them: they were in the rapids, while before them the white foam of the falls flashed through the darkness. The tide had ebbed in their absence, and the river, smooth and level when full, showed all across it, at the flood, a dark abyss of fearful rocks and boiling surf. This they knew, but it was now too late to recede; the dark stream bore them onward, and now even the Indians dare not follow, but landed and ran along the shore shouting with delight at their inevitable destruc-tion. It was a moment of dread, unutterable horror to Silas and his comrades. Their bark whirled round in the giddy waves--then was there a wild plunge--a fearful shock--a shriek of death, and the flashing foam gathered over them, while loudly rang the voices from the shore. But suddenly, by some mighty effort, the boat was flung clear of the rocks and uninjured into the smooth current of the lower stream. A few strokes of the oar brought them to the fort, which they entered; and heard the Indians howling behind them like wolves baffled of their prey. But they and the dangers they had so lately passed were alike forgotten in the night's carousal; and, when the season was ended, they returned to their homes in the settlements, enriched with the spoils they had gained in hunting, and Silas with his treasured pearl of the prairie.

But here, some months after they returned, and while, his heart was yet brightened with her smiles, a dark shade passed over her sunny brow, and she vanished from his home. An Indian of her tribe was said to have been lingering near the village, and she no doubt had joined him and returned to her kindred. Other tidings of her fate Silas heard not. Alas! she knew the undying vengeance of her people, and by giving herself up to them thought to shield him from their hatred.

Again the time of hunting came, and the same party occupied the fort in the wilderness. As yet they had been unmolested by the Indians: they even knew not of their being in the neighbourhood, yet still a form of guarding was kept up, and Silas and a comrade held the night-watch in the block house. The others had fallen asleep, and Silas, as he sat with half-closed eyes, fancied he saw before him his lost love, Leemah; he started as he thought from a dream, but 'twas real, and 'twas her own cool fingers pressed his brow--by the clear fire light he saw her cheek was deadly pale, but her eyes were flashing like sepulchral lamps, and a white-browed babe slept upon her bosom. In a deep thrilling whisper she bade him rise and follow her. Wondering how she had found entrance, he obeyed, and she led him outside the walls of the fort; a murmuring sound as of leaves stirred by the wind was heard.

'Tis the coming of the Red Eagle, said Leemah, his beak is whetted for the blood draughts; here enter, and if your own life or Leemah's be dear, keep still;--as she spoke she parted aside the young shoots which had sprung tip from the root of a tree, and twined like an arbour about it. Her deep earnestness left no time for speculation; he entered the recess, and hardly had the flexile boughs sprung back to their places, when the fleet footsteps of the Indians came nearer, and the fort was surrounded by them; the building was fired, and then their deadly yell burst forth, while the unfortunate inmates started from sleep at the sound of horror. Mercy for them there was none; the relentless savage knew it not; but the shout of delight rose louder as they saw the flames dance higher o'er their victims; and Silas looked on all--but Leemah's eye was on his--he knew his slightest movement was death to her as well as to himself. Like a demon through the flame leaped the ghastly form of the Red Eagle, (he to whom Leemah had been espoused) and with searching glance glared on his victims, but saw not there the one he sought with deeper vengeance than the others--'twas Silas he looked for; and, with the speed of a winged fiend, he bounded to where Leemah stood, and accused her of having aided in his escape. She acknowledged she had, and pointed to the far-off forest as his hiding place. In an instant his glittering tomahawk cleft the hand she raised off at the wrist. Silas knew no more. Leemah's hot blood fell upon his brow, and he fainted through excess of agony, but like Mazeppa, he lived to repay the Red Eagle in after-years for that night of horror--when his eyes had been blasted with the burning fort, his ears stunned with the shrieks of his murdered friends, and his brain scorched through with Leemah's life blood.

Long years after, when he had forsaken the hunter's path, and fought as a loyalist in the British ranks, among their Indian allies who smoked with them the pipe of peace and called them brothers, was one, in whose wild and withered features he recalled the stern Red Eagle; blood called for blood; he beguiled the Indian now with copious draughts of the white man's fire-water, and he and another (brother of one of the murdered hunters) killed him, and placing him in his own canoe with the paddle in his hand, sent the fearful corpse down the rapid stream, bearing him unto his home. The wild dog and wolf howled on the banks as it floated past, and the raven and eagle hovered over it claiming it as their prey. The tribe, at the death of their Sagamore, withdrew from their allies, and, following the track of the setting sun, waged war indiscriminately with all.

And long after, though more than half a century had elapsed since the death of the Red Eagle, and when the snows of eighty winters had whitened the dark tresses of the young hunter, and bowed the tall form of the loyalist soldier; when he who had trod the flowery paths of the prairie, and slept in the orchard bowers by the blue stream of the Hudson, had, for love of England's laws, become a refugee from his native land; and when here, in New Brunswick, he beheld raised around him a happy and comfortable home--his house, which had always been freely opened to religious worship, and in which had been held the prayer-meetings of the baptists and love-feasts of the methodists, became one day transformed into a catholic chapel.

A bishop of the Romish church was passing through the province, and his presence in this sequestered spot was an event of unwonted interest; many who had forgotten the creed of their fathers returned to the faith of their earlier days, and among the most fervent of those assembled, there was a small group of Milicete Indians from the woods hard by. With the idolatrous devotion of their half savage nature they fell prostrate before the priest. Among them was an ancient woman, but not of their tribe, who, while raising her head in prayer, or in crossing herself, Silas observed she used but one hand--the other was gone. This circumstance recalled to light the faded love-dream of his youth. He questioned her and found her to be Leemah, his once beautiful Indian bride, who had wandered here to escape the dark tyranny of her savage kindred. She died soon after, and "she sleeps there," said the old man, pointing to where a white cross marked a low grassy mound before us, and time had not so dried up his heart springs but I saw a tear drop to her memory.

     *   *   *   *   *

I turned my eyes from Leemah's grave to see what effect the tale had made on the old lady, but she was so engaged in contemplating the golden curls of her doughnuts, and feathery lightness of her pound cake, she had heard it not; and even if she had, it had all happened such a long time ago, that her impressions respecting it must all have worn out by now. After having partaken of the luxurious feast she set before us, and hearing some more of the old man's legends, we proceeded forward.

The evening, with one of those sudden changes of New Brunswick, had become cold and chilly. The sun looked red and lurid through the heavy masses of fog clouds drifting through the sky; this fog, which comes all the way from the Banks of Newfoundland, and which is particularly disagreeable sometimes along the Bay shore and in St. John, in opposition to the general clearness of the American atmosphere is but little known in the interior of the country. Numerous summer fallows are burning around, and the breeze flings over us showers of blackened leaves and blossoms. As we approached home, we were accosted by one Mr. Isaac Hanselpecker, a neighbour of ours; he was leaning over the bars, apparently wanting a lounge excessively. He had just finished milking, and had handed the pails to Miss Hanselpecker, as he called his wife. If there be a trait of American character peculiar to itself, displayed more fully than another by contrast with Europeans, it is in the treatment of the gentler sex, differing as it does materially from the picture of the Englishman, standing with his back to the fire, while the ladies freeze around him; or the glittering politeness of the Frenchman, hovering like a butterfly by the music stand; it has in it more of intellect and real tenderness than either, although tending as it does to the advancement of national character, some of their own talented ones begin to complain that in the refined circles of the States they are becoming almost too civilised in this respect: the ladies requiring rather more than is due to them. Yet among the working classes it has a sweet and wholesome influence, softening as it does the asperities of labour, and lightening the burthen to each. Here woman's empire is within, and here she shines the household star of the poor man's hearth; not in idleness, for in America, of all countries in the world, prosperity depends on female industry. Here "she looketh well to the ways of her household, and eateth not the bread of idleness," and for this reason, perhaps, it is, that their husbands arise and call them blessed. Now Mr. Hanselpecker had all the respect for his lady natural to his country, and assisted her domestic toils by milking the cows, making fires, and fetching wood and water. Yet there was one material point in which he failed: she was often "scant of bread," he being one who, even in this land of toil, got along, somehow or other, with wondrous little bodily labour; professing to be a farmer, he held one of the finest pieces of land in the settlement, but his agricultural operations, for the most part, consisted in hoeing a few sickly stems of corn, while others were reaping buckwheat, or sowing a patch of flax, "'cause the old woman wanted loom gears;" shooting cranes, spearing salmon, or trapping musquash on the lake, he prefers to raising fowl or sheep, as cranes find their own provisions, and fish require no fences to keep them from the fields. His wife's skill, however, in managing the dairy department, is, when butter rates well in the market, their chief dependence; and he, when he chooses to work, which he would much rather do for another than himself, can earn enough in one day, if he take truck, to keep him three, and but that he prefers fixing cucumbers to thrashing, and making moccasins to clearing land, he might do well enough. Though poor, he is none the least inclined to grovel, but, with the spirit of his land, feels quite at ease in company with any judge or general in the country.

Having declined his invitation to enter the log erection,--which in another country would hardly be styled a house, he having still delayed to enclose the gigantic frame, whose skeleton form was reared hard by--he gave his opinion of the weather at present, with some shrewd guesses as to what it would be in future; regarding the smoke wreaths from the fires around (there were none on his land however), he said, it reminded him of the fire in Miramichi. "How long is it, old woman," said he, turning to his wife, who had now joined us, "since that ere burning?" "Well," said she, "I aint exactly availed to tell you right off how many years it is since, but I guess our Jake was a week old when it happened."

Now, as the burning of Miramichi was one of the most interesting historical events in the province records, we gave him the date, which was some twenty years since; this also gave us the sum of Jacob's lustres--rather few considering he had planted a tater patch on shares, and laid out to marry in the fall.

"Well," said he, "You may depend that was a fire--my hair curls yet when I think of it--it was the same summer we got married, and Washington Welford having been out a timber-hunting with me the fall afore, we discovered a most elegant growth of pine--I never see'd before nor since the equal on it--regular sixty footers, every log on 'em--the trees stood on the banks of the river, as if growing there on purpose to be handy for rafting, and we having got a first-rate supply from our merchants in town, toted our things with some of the old woman's house trumpery to the spot--we soon had up a shanty, and went to work in right airnest. There was no mistake in Wash; he was as clever a fellow as ever I knowed, and as handsome a one--seven feet without his shoes--eyes like diamonds, and hair slick as silk; when he swung his axe among the timber, you may depend he looked as if he had a mind to do it--our felling and hewing went on great, and with the old woman for cook we made out grand--she, however, being rather delicate, we hired a help, a daughter of a neighbour about thirty miles off. Ellen Ross was as smart a gal as ever was raised in these clearings--her parents were old country folks, and she had most grand larning, and was out and out a regular first-rater. Washington and her didn't feel at all small together--they took a liking to each other right away, and a prettier span was never geared. Well, our Jake was born, and the old woman got smart, and about house again. Wash took one of our team horses, and he and Ellen went off to the squire's to get yoked. It was a most beautiful morning when they started, but the weather soon began to change--there had been a most uncommon dry spell--not a drop of rain for many weeks, nor hardly a breath of air in the woods, but now there came a most fearful wind and storm, and awful black clouds gathering through the sky--the sun grew blood red, and looked most terrible through the smoke. I had heard of such things as 'clipses, but neither the almanac, nor the old woman's universal, said a word about it. Altho' there was such a wind, there was the most burning heat--one could hardly breathe, and the baby lay pale and gasping--we thought it was a dying. The cattle grew oneasy, and all at once a herd of moose bounded into our chopping, and a lot of bears after them, all running as if for dear life. I got down the rifle, and was just a going to let fly at them, when a scream from the old woman made me look about. The woods were on fire all round us, and the smoke parting before us, showed the flames crackling and roaring like mad, 'till the very sky seemed on fire over our heads. I did'nt know what to do, and, in fact, there was no time to calculate about it. The blaze glared hotly on our faces, and all the wild critturs of the woods began to carry on most ridiculous, and shout and holler like all nature I caught up my axe, and the old woman the baby, and took the only open space left for us, where the stream was running, and the fire couldn't catch. Just as we were going, a horse came galloping most awful fast right through the fire--it was poor Washington; his clothes all burnt, and his black hair turned white as snow, and oh! the fearful burden he carried in his arms. Ellen Ross, the beautiful bright-eyed girl, who had left us so smilingly in the morning, lay now before us a scorched and blackened corpse--the scared horse fell dead on the ground. I hollered to Washington to follow us to the water, but he heard me not; and the flames closed fast o'er him and his dead bride--poor fellow, that was the last on him--and creation might be biled down, ere you could ditto him any how. By chance our timber was lying near in the stream, and I got the old woman and the baby on a log, and stood beside them up to the neck in water, which now grew hot, and actilly began to hiss around me. The trees on the other side of the river had caught, and there was an arch of flame right above us. My stars! what a time we had of it! Lucifees and minks, carraboo and all came close about us, and an Indian devil got upon the log beside my wife; poor critturs, they were all as tame as possible, and half frightened to death. I thought the end of the world was come for sartain. I tried to pray, but I was got so awful hungry, that grace before meat was all I could think off. How long we had been there I couldn't tell, but it seemed tome a 'tarnity--fire, howsomever, cannot burn always--that's a fact; so at the end of what we afterwards found to be the third day, we saw the sun shine down on the still smoking woods. The old woman was weak, I tell you; and for me, I felt considerably used up--howsomever I got to the shore, and hewed out a canoe from one of our own timber sticks--there was no need of lucifers to strike a light--lots of brands were burning about. I laid some on to it and burnt it out, and soon had a capital craft, and away we went down the stream. Dead bodies of animals were floating about, and there were some living ones, look-ing as if they had got out of their latitude, and didn't think they would find it. I reckon we weren't the only sufferers by that ere conflagration. As we came down to the settlements folks took us for ghosts, we looked so miserable like--howsomever, with good tendin, we soon came round again; but, to tell you the truth, it makes me feel kind a narvous, when I see a fallow burning ever since. Tho' folks could'nt tell how that ere fire happened, and say it was a judgment on lumber men and sich like, I think it came from some settlers' improvements, who, wishing to raise lots of taters, destroyed the finest block of timber land in the province, besides the ships in Miramichi harbour, folks' buildings, and many a clever feller, whose latter end was never known."

"And so I suppose Mr. H.," said his wife, "that is the reason you make such slim clearings." "I estimate your right," said he; and we, not expecting the spice of senti-ment which flavored Mr. H.'s story, left him, and reached home, where we closed the evening by putting into the following shape one of Silas Marvin's legends, not written with a perryian pen and azure fluid, but with a quill from the wing of a wild goose, shot by our friend Hanselpecker, (who by the way was fond of such game,) as last fall it took its flight from our cold land to the sunny south, and with home-made ink prepared from a decoction of white maple bark.

THE LOST ONE,
A TALE OF THE EARLY SETTLERS.

Beyond the utmost verge of the limits which the white settlers had yet dared to encroach on the red owners of the soil, stood the humble dwelling of Kenneth Gor-don, a Scotch emigrant, whom necessity had driven from the blue hills and fertile vallies of his native land, to seek a shelter in the tangled mazes of the forests of the new world. Few would have had the courage to venture thus into the very power of the savage--but Kenneth Gordon possessed a strong arm and a hopeful heart, to give the lips he loved unborrowed bread; this nerved him against danger, and, 'spite of the warning of friends, Kenneth pitched his tent twelve miles from the nearest settlement. Two years passed over the family in their lonely home, and nothing had occurred to disturb their peace, when business required Kenneth's presence up the river. One calm and dewy morning he prepared for his journey; Marion Gordon followed her husband to the wicket, and a tear, which she vainly strove to hide with a smile, trembled in her large blue eye. She wedded Kenneth when she might well have won a richer bridegroom: she chose him for his worth; their lot had been a hard one--but in all the changing scenes of life their love remained unchanged; and Kenneth Gordon, although thirteen years a husband, was still a lover. Marion strove to rally her spirits, as her husband gaily cheered her with an assurance of his return before night. "Why so fearful, Marion? See here is our ain bonny Charlie for a guard, and what better could an auld Jacobite wish for?" said Kenneth, looking fondly on his wife; while their son marched past them in his Highland dress and wooden claymore by his side. Marion smiled as her husband playfully alluded to the difference in their religion; for Kenneth was a staunch presbyterian, and his wife a Roman catholic; yet that difference--for which so much blood has been shed in the world--never for an instant dimmed the lustre of their peace; and Marion told her glittering beads on the same spot where her husband breathed his simple prayer. Kenneth, taking advantage of the smile he had roused, waved his hand to the little group, and was soon out of sight.

The hot and sultry day was passed by Marion in a state of restless anxiety, but it was for Kenneth alone she feared, and the hours sped heavily till she might expect his return. Slowly the burning sun declined in the heavens, and poured a flood of golden radiance on the leafy trees and the bright waves of the majestic river, which rolled its graceful waters past the settlers dwelling. Marion left her infant asleep in a small shed at the back of the log-house, with Mary, her eldest daughter, to watch by it, and taking Charlie by the hand went out to the gate to look for her husband's return. Kenneth's father, an old and almost superannuated man, sat in the door-way, with twin girls of Kenneth's sitting on his knees, singing their evening hymn, while he bent fondly over them.

Scarcely had Marion reached the wicket, when a loud yell--the wild war-whoop of the savage--rang on her startled ear. A thousand dark figures seemed to start from the water's edge--the house was surrounded, and she beheld the grey hairs of the old man twined round in the hand of one, and the bright curls of her daughters gleamed in that of another; while the glittering tomahawk glared like lightning in her eyes. Madly she rushed forward to shield her children; the vengeance of the Indian was glutted, and the life-blood of their victims crimsoned the hearth stone! The house was soon in flames--the war dance was finished--and their canoes bounded lightly on the waters, bearing them far from the scene of their havoc.

As the sun set a heavy shower of rain fell and refreshed the parched earth--the flowers sent up a grateful fragrance on the evening air--the few singing birds of the woods poured forth their notes of melody--the blue jay screamed among the crimson buds of the maple, and the humming bird gleamed through the emerald sprays of the beech tree.

The pearly moon was slowly rising in the blue aether, when Kenneth Gordon approached his home. He was weary with his journey, but the pictured visions of his happy home, his smiling wife, and the caresses of his sunny haired children, cheered the father's heart, though his step was languid, and his brow feverish. But oh! what a sight of horror for a fond and loving heart met his eyes, as he came in sight of the spot that contained his earthly treasures--the foreboding silence had surprised him--he heard not the gleeful voices of his children, as they were wont to bound forth to meet him, he saw not Marion stand at the gate to greet his return--but a thick black smoke rose heavily to the summits of the trees, and the smouldering logs of the building fell with a sullen noise to the ground. The rain had quenched the fire, and the house was not all consumed. Wild with terror, Kenneth rushed forward; his feet slipped on the bloody threshhold, and he fell on the mangled bodies of his father and his children. The demoniac laceration of the stiffening victims told too plainly who had been their murderers. How that night of horror passed Kenneth knew not. The morning sun was shining bright--when the bereaved and broken-hearted man was roused from the stupor of despair by the sound of the word "father" in his ears; he raised his eyes, and beheld Mary, his eldest daughter, on her knees beside him. For a moment Kenneth fancied he had had a dreadful dream, but the awful reality was before him. He pressed Mary wildly to his bosom, and a passionate flood of tears relieved his burning brain. Mary had heard the yells of the savages, and the shrieks of her mother convinced her that the dreaded Indians had arrived. She threw open the window, and snatching the infant from its bed, flew like a wounded deer to the woods behind the house. The frightened girl heard all, remained quiet, and knowing her father would soon return, left the little Alice asleep on some dried leaves, and ventured from her hiding place.

No trace of Marion or of Charles could be found--they had been reserved for a worse fate; and for months a vigilant search was kept up--parties of the settlers, led on by Kenneth, scoured the woods night and day. Many miles off a bloody battle had been fought between two hostile tribes, where a part of Marion's dress and of her son's was found, but here all trace of the Indians ended, and Kenneth returned to his desolated home. No persuasion could induce him to leave the place where the joys of his heart had been buried: true, his remaining children yet linked him to life, but his love for them only increased his sorrow for the dead and the lost. Kenneth became a prematurely old man--his dark hair faded white as the mountain snow-- his brow was wrinkled, and his tall figure bent downwards to the earth.

Seventeen years had rolled on their returnless flight since that night of withering sorrow. Kenneth Gordon still lived, a sad and broken-spirited man; but time, that great tamer of the human heart, which dulls the arrows of affliction, and softens the bright tints of joy down to a sober hue, had shed its healing influence even over his wounded heart. Mary Gordon had been some years a wife, and her children played around Kenneth's footsteps. A little Marion recalled the wife of his youth; and another, Charlie, the image of his lost son, slept in his bosom. There was yet another person who was as a sunbeam in the sight of Kenneth; her light laugh sounded as music in his ears, and the joy-beams of her eyes fell gladly on his soul. This gladdener of sorrow was his daughter Alice, now a young and lovely woman; bright and beautiful was she, lovely as a rose-bud, with a living soul--

"No fountain from its native cave,
E'er tripped with foot so free;
She was as happy as a wave

That dances o'er the sea."

Alice was but five months old when her mother was taken from her, but Mary, who watched over her helpless infancy with a care far beyond her years, and with love equal to a mother's, was repaid by Alice with most unbounded affection; for to the love of a sister was added the veneration of a parent.

One bright and balmy Sabbath morning Kenneth Gordon and his family left their home for the house of prayer. Mary and her husband walked together, and their children gambolled on the grassy path before them. Kenneth leaned on the arm of his daughter Alice; another person walked by her side, whose eye, when it met her's, deepened the tint on her fair cheek. It was William Douglas--the chosen lover of her heart, and well worthy was he to love the gentle Alice. Together they proceeded to the holy altar, and the next Sabbath was to be their bridal day.

A change had taken place since Kenneth Gordon first settled on the banks of the lonely river. The white walls and graceful spire of a church now rose where the blue smoke of the solitary log-house once curled through the forest trees; and the ashes of Kenneth's children and his father reposed within its sacred precincts. A large and populous village stood where the red deer roved on his trackless path. The white sails of the laden barque gleamed on the water, where erst floated the stealthy canoe of the savage; and a pious throng offered their aspirations where the war-whoop had rung on the air.

Alice was to spend the remaining days of her maiden life with a young friend, a few miles from her father's, and they were to return together on her bridal eve. William Douglas accompanied Alice on her walk to the house of her friend. They parted within a few steps of the house. William returned home, and Alice, gay and gladsome as a bird, entered a piece of wood, which led directly to the house. Scarcely had she entered it when she was seized by a strong arm; her mouth was gagged, and something thrown over her head; she was then borne rapidly down the bank of the river, and laid in a canoe. She heard no voices, and the swift motion of the canoe rendered her unconscious. How long the journey lasted she knew not. At length she found herself, on recovering from partial insensibility, in a rude hut, with a frightful-looking Indian squaw bathing her hands, while another held a blazing torch of pine above her head. Their hideous faces, frightful as the imagery of a dream, scared Alice, and she fainted again.

The injuries which Kenneth Gordon had suffered from the savages made him shudder at the name of Indian--and neither he nor his family ever held converse with those who traded in the village. Metea, a chief of the Menomene Indians, in his frequent trading expeditions to the village, had often seen Alice, and became enamoured of the village beauty. He had long watched an opportunity of stealing her, and bearing her away to his tribe, where he made no doubt of winning her love. When Alice recovered the squaws left her, and Metea entered the hut; he commenced by telling her of the great honour in being allowed to share the hut of Metea, a "brave" whose bow was always strung, whose tomahawk never missed its blow, and whose scalps were as numerous as the stars in the path-way of ghosts; and he pointed to the grisly trophies hung in the smoke of the cabin. He concluded by giving her furs and strings of beads, with which the squaws decorated her, and the next morning the trembling girl was led from the hut, and lifted into a circle formed of the warriors of the tribe. Here Metea stood forth and declared his deeds of bravery, and asked their consent for "the flower of the white nation" to be his bride. When he had finished, a young warrior, whose light and graceful limbs might well have been a sculptor's model, stood forward to speak. He was dressed in the richest Indian costume, and his scalping knife and beaded moccasins glittered in the sunshine. His features bore an expression very different from the others. Neither malice nor cunning lurked in his full dark eye, but a calm and majestic melancholy reposed on his high and smooth brow, and was diffused over his whole mein; and, in the clear tones of his voice, "Brothers," said he to the warriors, "we have buried the hatchet with the white nation--it is very deep beneath the earth--shall we dig it because Metea scorns the women of his tribe, because he has stolen 'the flower of the white nation?' Let her be restored to her people, lest her chiefs come to claim her, and Metea lives to disgrace the brave warriors of the woods?" He sat down, and the circle rising, said, "Our brother speaks well, but Metea is very ***brave***." It was decided that Alice should remain.

Towards evening Metea entered the hut, and approaching Alice, caught hold of her hand,--the wildest passion gleamed in his glittering eyes, and Alice, shrieking, ran towards the door. Metea caught her in his arms and pressed her to his bosom. Again she shrieked, and a descending blow cleft Metea's skull in sunder, and his blood fell on her neck. It was the young Indian who advised her liberation in the morning who dealt Metea's death-blow. Taking Alice in his arms, he stepped lightly from the hut. It was a still and starless night, and the sleeping Indians saw them not. Unloosing a canoe, he placed Alice in it, and pushed softly from the shore.

Before the next sunset Alice was in sight of her home. Her father and friends knew nothing of what had transpired. They fancied her at her friend's house, and terror at her peril and joy at her return followed in the same breath. Mary threw a timid, yet kind glance on the Indian warrior who had saved her darling Alice, and Kenneth pressed the hand of him who restored his child. In a few minutes William Douglas joined the happy group, and she repeated her escape on his bosom. That night Kenneth Gordon's prayer was longer and more fervent than usual. The father's thanks arose to the throne of grace for the safety of his child; he prayed for her deliverer, and for pardon for the hatred he had nurtured against the murderers of his children. During the prayer the Indian stood apart, his arms were folded, and deep thought was marked on his brow. When it was finished, Mary's children knelt and received Kenneth's blessing, ere they retired to rest. The Indian rushed forward, and, bursting into tears, threw himself at the old man's feet--he bent his feathered head to the earth. The stern warrior wept like a child. Oh! who can trace the deep workings of the human heart? Who can tell in what hidden fount the feelings have their spring? The forest chase--the bloody field--the war dance--all the pomp of savage life passed like a dream from the Indian's soul; a cloud seemed to roll its shadows from his memory. That evening's prayer, and a father's blessing, recalled a time faded from his recollection, yet living in the dreams of his soul. He thought of the period when he, a happy child like those before him, had knelt and heard the same sweet words breathed o'er his bending head: he remembered having received a father's kiss, and a mother's smile gleamed like a star in his memory; but the fleeting visions of childhood were fading again into darkness, when Kenneth arose, and, clasping the Indian wildly to his breast, exclaimed, "My son, my son! my long lost Charles!" The springs of the father's love gushed forth to meet his son, and the unseen sympathy of nature guided him to "The Lost One." 'Twas indeed Charles Gordon, whom his father held to his breast, but not as he lived in his father's fancy. He beheld him a painted savage, whose hand was yet stained with blood; but Kenneth's fondest prayer was granted, and he pressed him again to his bosom, exclaiming again, "He is my son." A small gold cross hung suspended from the collar of Charles. Kenneth knew it well; it had belonged to Marion, who hung it round her son's neck e'er her eyes were closed. She had sickened early of her captivity, and died while her son was yet a child: but the relics she had left were prized by him as something holy. From his wampum belt he took a roll of the bark of the birch tree, on which something had been written with a pencil. The writing was nearly effaced, and the signature of Marion Gordon was alone distinguishable. Kenneth pressed the writing to his lips, and again his bruised spirit mourned for his sainted Marion. Mary and Alice greeted their restored brother with warm affection. Kenneth lived but in the sight of his son. Charles rejoiced in their endearments, and all the joys of kindred were to him

> "New as if brought from other spheres,
> Yet welcome as if known for years."

But soon a change came o'er the young warrior; his eye grew dim, his step was heavy, and his brow was sad: he sought for solitude, and he seemed like a bird pining for freedom. They thought he sighed for the liberty of his savage life, but, alas! it was another cause. The better feelings of the human heart all lie dormant in the Indian character, and are but seldom called into action. Charles had been the "stern stoic of the woods" till he saw Alice. Then the first warm rush of young affections bounded like a torrent through his veins, and he loved his sister with a passion so strong, so overwhelming, that it sapped the current of his life. The marriage of Alice had been delayed on his return--it would again have been delayed on his account, but he himself urged it forward. Kenneth entered the church with Charles leaning on his arm. During the ceremony he stood apart from the others. When it was finished, Alice went up to him and took his hand; it was cold as marble--he was dead; his spirit fled with the bridal benediction. Kenneth's heart bled afresh for his son, and as he laid his head in the earth he felt that it would not be long till he followed him. Nor was he mistaken; for a few mornings after he was found dead on the grave of "*The Lost One*."

    *   *   *   *   *

And now the bright summer of New Brunswick drew onward to its close. The hay, which in this country is cut in a much greener state than is usual elsewhere, and which, from this cause, retains its fragrance till the spring, was safely lodged in the capacious barns. The buck wheat had changed its delicate white flower for the brown clusters of its grain, and the reaper and the thrasher were both busied with it, for so loosely does this grain hang on its stem that it is generally thrashed out of doors as soon as ripe, as much would be lost in the conveyance to the barn.

Grace Marley's time of departure now drew near; her government stipend had arrived. The proprietors, who paid in trade, had deposited the butter and oats equivalent to her hire in the market boat, in which she intended to proceed to town. And as this is decidedly the pleasantest method of travelling, I laid out to accompany her by the same conveyance, and we were spending the last evening with Mrs. Gordon, who also was to be our companion to St. John; we walked with Helen through her flower-garden, who showed us some flowers, the seeds of which she had received from the old country. I saw a bright hue pass o'er the brow of Grace as we walked among them, and tears gushed forth from her warm and feeling heart. Next day she explained what occasioned her emotion, a feeling which all must have felt, awakened by as slight a cause, when wandering far from their native land. Thus she pourtrayed what she then felt--

THE MIGNIONETTE.

'Twas when the summer's golden eve
Fell dim o'er flower and fruit,
A mystic spell was o'er me thrown,
As I'd drank of some charmed root.
It came o'er my soul as the breeze swept by,
Like the breath of some blessed thing;
Again it came, and my spirit rose
As if borne on an angel's wing.
It bore me away to my native land,
Away o'er the deep sea foam;

And I stood, once more a happy child,
By the hearth of my early home.
And well-loved forms were by me there,
That long in the grave had lain;
And I heard the voices I heard of old,
And they smiled on me again.
And I knew once more the dazzling light,
Of the spirit's gladsome youth;
And lived again in the sunny light
Of the heart's unbroken truth.
Yet felt I then, as we always feel,
The sweet grief o'er me cast,
When a chord is waked of the spirit's harp,
Which telleth of the past.
And what could it be, that blissful trance?
What caused the soul to glide?
Forgetting alike both time and change,
So far o'er memory's tide.
Oh! could that deep mysterious power
Be but the breath of an earthly flower?
'Twas not the rose with her leaves so bright,
That flung o'er my soul such dazzling light,
Nor the tiger lily's gorgeous dies,
That changed the hue of my spirit's eyes.
'Twas not from the pale, but gifted leaf,
That bringeth to mortal pain relief.
Not where the blue wreaths of the star-flower shine,
Nor lingered it in the airy bells
Of the graceful columbine.
But again it cometh, I breathe it yet,
'Tis the sigh of the lowly mignionette.
And there, 'mid the garden's leafy gems,
Blossomed a group of its fairy stems;

Few would have thought of its faint perfume,
While they gazed on the rosebud's crimson bloom.
But to me it was laden with sighs and tears,
And the faded hopes of by-gone years.
Many a vision, long buried deep,
Was waked again from its dreamless sleep.
Thoughts whose light was dim before,
Lived in their pristine truth once more.
Well might its form with my fancies weave,
For in youth it seemed with me to joy,
And in woe with me to grieve.
Oft have I knelt in the cool moonlight,
Where it wreathed the lattice pane,
'Till I felt that He who formed the flower
Would hear my prayer again.
Then, welcome sweet thing, in this stranger land,
May it smile upon thy birth,
Light fall the rain on thy lovely head,
And genial be the earth;
And blest be the power that gave to thee,
All lowly as thou art,
The gift unknown to prouder things,
To soothe and teach the heart.

Next day we proceeded on our journey, and, preferring the coolness of the deck
to the heated atmosphere of the cabin, seated ourselves there to enjoy the quiet
beauty of the night. The full glory of a September's moon was beaming bright in the
clear rich blue of heaven; the stars were glittering in the water's depths, and ever
and anon the fire flies flashed like diamonds through the dark foliage on the shore--
the light fair breeze scarce stirred the ripples on the stream--when, from one of the
white dwellings on the beach in whose casement a light was yet burning, came a
low, sad strain of sorrow. I had heard that sound once before, and knew now it was
the wail of Irish grief. Strange that mournful dirge of Erin sounded in that distant

land. Grace knew the language of her country, and ere the "keen" had died upon the breeze, she translated thus

THE SONG OF THE IRISH MOURNER.

Light of the widow's heart! art thou then dead?
And is then thy spirit from earth ever fled?
And shall we, then, see thee and hear thee no more,
All radiant in beauty and life as before?

My own blue-eyed darling, Oh, why didst thou die,
Ere the tear-drop of sorrow had dimmed thy bright eye,
Ere thy cheek's blooming hue felt one touch of decay,
Or thy long golden ringlets were mingled with grey?

Why, star of our path-way, why didst thou depart?
Why leave us to weep for the pulse of the heart?
Oh, darkened for ever is life's sunny hour,
When robbed of its brightest and loveliest flower!

Around thy low bier sacred incense is flinging,
And soft on the air are the silver bells ringing;
For the peace of thy soul is the holy mass said,
And on thy fair forehead the blessed cross laid.

Soft, soft be thy slumbers, our lady receive thee,
And shining in glory for ever thy soul be;
To the climes of the blessed, my own grama-chree,
May blessings attend thee, sweet cushla ma-chree.

As we passed the jemseg, we spoke of the time when Madame la Tour so bravely defended the fort in the absence of her husband--this occurred in the early times of the province, and strange stories are told of spirit forms which glide along the beach, beneath whose sands the white bones of the French and Indians, who fell in the deadly fight, lie buried. Talking of these things, induced Mrs. Gordon to tell us the following tale, which she had heard, and which I have entitled

A WINTER'S EVENING SKETCH, WRITTEN IN NEW BRUNSWICK.

"Oh! there's a dream of early youth,
And it never comes again;
'Tis a vision of joy, and light, and truth,
That flits across the brain;
And love is the theme of that early dream,
So wild, so warm, so new.
And oft I ween, in our after-years,
That early dream we rue."---Mrs. HEMANS.

The winter's eve had gathered o'er New Brunswick, and the snow was falling, as in that clime it only knows how to fall. The atmosphere was like the face of Sterne's monk, "calm, cold, and penetrating," and the faint tinkling of the sleigh bells came mournfully on the ear as a knell of sadness--so utterly cheerless was the scene. Another hour passed, and our journey was ended. The open door of the hospitable dwelling was ready to receive us, and in the light and heat of a happy home, toil and trouble were alike forgotten.

There is always something picturesque in the interior of a New Brunswick farm house, and this evening everything assumed an aspect of interest and beauty. It might have been the comfortable contrast to the scene without that threw its mellow tints around. Even the homely loom and spinning-wheel lost their uncouthness, and recalled to the mind's imagery the classic dreams of old romance--Hercules in the chambers of Omphale the story of Arachne and Penelope, the faithful wife of brave Ulysses; but there was other food for the spirit which required not the aid of fancy to render palatable. On the large centre table, round which were grouped the household band, with smiling brows and happy hearts, lay the magazines and papers of the day, with their sweet tales and poetic gems. The "Amulet" and "Keepsake" glittering in silk and gold, and "Chambers," with plain, unwinning exterior, the ungarnished casket of a mine of treasure, gave forth, like whisperings from a better land, their gentle influence to soothe and cheer the heart, and teach the spirit higher aspirations, while breathing the magic spells raised by their fairy power--those sweet creators of a world unswayed by earth, where hope and beauty live undimmed by time or tears--givers to all who own their power, a solace 'mid the pining cares of life. Thus, with the aid of these, and the joys of converse, sped the night; and as the wind which had now arisen blew heavy gusts of frozen rain against the windows, we rejoiced in our situation all the more, and looked complacently on the great mainspring of our comfort, the glowing stove, which imparted its grateful caloric through the apartment, and bore on its polished surface shining evidence of the housewife's care. 'Twas apparently already a favourite, and the storm without had enhanced its value. Without dissent, all agreed in its perfection and superiority over ordinary fire-places.

Twas a theme which called forth conversation, and when all had given their opinion, uncle Ethel was asked for his.

The person so addressed was an aged man, who reclined in an arm chair apart from the others, sharing not in words with their discourse or mirth, but smiling like a benignant spirit on them. More than eighty years of shade and sunshine had passed o'er him. The few snowy locks which lingered yet around his brow were soft and silky as a child's--time and sorrow had traced him but a gentle path, 'twould seem by the light which yet beamed in his calm blue eye and placid smile, the expression was far different from mirthful happiness, but breathed of holy peace and spirit pure, tempered with love and kindness for all--living in the past dreams of youth, he loved the present, when it recalled their sweet memories in brighter beauty from the tomb of faded years, and then it seemed as if a secret woe arose and dimmed the vision when it glowed brightest. A deeper sorrow than for departed youth flashed o'er his brow, brief but fearful, as though he once, and but once only, had felt a pang of agony which had deadened all other lighter woes, and, overcome by resignation, left the spirit calmer as its strong feeling passed away. Such was what we knew of uncle Ethel, but ere the night had worn we knew him better. Joining us in our conversation regarding the stove, he smiled, and said he agreed not with us-- our favourite was more sightly, and more useful, but it bore not the friendly face of the old hearthstone--one of memory's most treasured spots was gone--the *fireside* of our home--the thought of whose hallowed precincts cheers the wanderer's heart, and has won many from the path of error, to seek again its sinless welcome.

'Tis while sitting by the fireside at eve, said he, that the vanished forms of other days gather round me--there where our happiest meetings were in the holy sanctity of our **home**. Where peace and love hovered o'er us, I see again kind faces lit by the ruddy gleam, and hear again the evening hymn, as of old it used to rise from the loving band assembled there. Alas! long years have passed since I missed them from the earth, but there they meet me still--in the glowing fire's bright light I trace their sweet names, and the vague fancies of childhood are waked again from their dim repose to live in light and truth once more, amid the fantastic visions and shadowy forms, flitting through the red world of embers, on which I loved to gaze when thought and hope were young. I love it even now--the sorrow that is written there makes it more holy to my mind, telling me, as it does, of a clime where grief comes not, and where the blighted hope and broken heart will be at rest.

But why, said the old man, do I talk so long--I weary you, my children, for the fancies of age are not those of youth--hope's fairy flowers are bright for you--the faded things of memory are mine alone--with them I live, but rejoice ye in your happiness, and gather now, in the spring time of your days, treasures to cheer you in the fall of life. As to your favourite, the stove, although I love it not so well as the old familiar fire-place, I can admire and value it as part of the spirit of improve- ment which is spreading o'er our land--her early troubles are passing away, and she is rising fast to take her place among the nations of the earth--bitter has been her struggle for existence, but the clouds are fading in the brightness of her coming years, and her past woes will be forgotten.

He ceased, but we all loved to hear him talk, he was so kind and good, and he was earnestly requested for one of those tales of the early times of our own land, which had often thrilled us with their simple, yet often woeful interest.

I am become an egotist to-night, for self is the only theme of which I can discourse. My spirit, too, is like the minstrel harp of which you have to-night been reading, 'twill "echo nought but sadness;" but if it please you, you shall have uncle Ethel's love story--well may we say alas! for time,

> "For he taketh away the heart of youth,
> And its gladness which hath been
> Like the summer's sunshine on our path,
> Making the desert green."

More than sixty years have elapsed since the time of which I now shall speak. We lived then, a large and happy family, in the dwelling where our fathers' sires had died--sons and daughters had married, but still remained beneath the shadow of the parent roof tree, which seemed to extend its wings like a guardian spirit, as they increased in number. 'Twas near the city of New York, and stood in the centre of sunny fields, which had been won from the forest shade. Our parents were natives of the soil, but theirs had come from the far land of Germany, and the memories of that land were still fondly cherished by their descendants. The low-roofed cottage, with its many-pointed gables and narrow casement, was gay with the bright flowers of that home of their hearts--cherished and guarded there with the tenderest care--all hues of earth seemed blended in the bright parterre of tulips, over which the magnificent dahlia towered, tall and stately as a queen--the rich scent of the wallflower breathed around, and the jessamine went climbing freely o'er the trellissed porch and arching eaves--each flower around my home bore to me the face of a friend--they bore to me the poetry of the earth, as the stars tell the sweet harmonies of heaven--but there is a vision of fairer beauty than either star or flower comes with the thought of these bye-gone days--the face of my orphan cousin Ella Werner arises in the brightness of its young beauty, as it used to beam upon me from the latticed window of my home: for her's, indeed,

> "Was a form of life and light,
> That seen became a part of sight,
> And comes where'er I turn mine eye,
> The morning star of memory."

Ella's mother was sister to my father: she lived but long enough to look upon her child, and her husband died of a broken heart soon after her. Thus the very existence of the fair girl was fatal to those who best loved her--not best, for all living loved her. In after-years it seemed as though it was her beauty, that fatal gift, which ne'er for good was given to many, caused her woe. Ella's spirit was pure and bright as the eyes through which it beamed--the gladness of her young heart's happiness rung in the silvery music of her voice, and in the fairy magic of her smile she looked as if sorrow could never dim the golden lustre of her curls, or trace a cloud on her snowy brow--gentle and lovely she was, and that was all. There was no depth of thought, no strength of mind, to form the character of one so gifted. Her faculties for reasoning were the impulses of her own heart: these were generally good, and constituted her principle of action--but changeful as the summer sky are the feelings of the human heart, unswayed by the deeper power of the head. Such were Ella's, and their power destroyed her. Alas! how calmly can I talk now of her faults; but who could think of them when they looked upon her, and loved her as I did-- 'tis only since she is gone I discover them.

Of the other members of the family I need not speak, as you already know of them; but there is one whose name you have never heard, for crime and sorrow rest with it, and oblivion shrouds his memory. Conrad Ernstein was also my cousin, and an orphan--he was an inmate of our dwelling, and my mother was to him as a parent. He was some years older, but his delicate constitution and studious mind withdrew him from the others, and made him the companion of Ella and myself. I have said that Ella's mind was too volatile, so in like degree was Conrad's, in its deep unchanging firmness and immutability of purpose. Nothing deterred him from the pursuit of any object he engaged in--obstacles but increased his energy to overcome and call forth stronger powers of mind--this was observable in his learning. Science the most abstruse and difficult was his favourite study, and in these he attained an excellence rarely arrived at by one so situated.

Wondered at and admired by all, his pride which was great was amply gratified, and what was evil in his nature was not yet called into being--his disposition was melancholy, and showed none of the joyousness of youth--yet that very sadness seemed to make us love him all the more--his air of suffering asked for pity--'twas strange to see the glad-hearted Ella leave my mother's side, while she sang to us the songs of the blue Rhine, and bend her sunny brow with him over the ancient page of some clasped volume, containing the terrific legends of the "black forest," till the tales of the wild huntsmen filled her with dread--then again would she spring to my mother, and burying her head in her bosom, ask her once more to sing the songs of her native land, for so we still called Germany; and, as you see, the romances and legends of that country formed our childhood's lore, my early love for Ella grew and increased with my years, and I fancied that she loved me.

On the first of May, or, as it was by us styled, "Walburga's eve," the young German maidens have a custom of seeking a lonely stream, and flinging on its waters a wreath of early flowers, as an offering to a spirit which then has power. When, as the legend tells, the face of their lover will glide along the water, and the name be borne on the breeze, if the gift be pleasing to the spirit. Ella, I knew, had for some time been preparing to keep this ancient relic of the pagan rites--she had a treasured rose tree which bloomed, unexpectedly, early in the season--these delicate things she fancied would be a fitting offering to the spirit. She paused not to think of what she was about to do--the thing itself was but a harmless folly--from aught of ill her nature would have drawn instinctively; but evil there might have been-- she stayed not to weigh the result--at the last hour of sunset she wreathed her roses, and set out. In the lightness of my heart I followed in the same path, intending to surprize her. I heard her clear voice floating on the air, as she sung the invocation to the spirit--the words were these:--

> Blue-eyed spirit of balmy spring,
> Bright young flowers to thee I bring,
> Wreaths all tinged with hues divine,
> Meet to rest on thy fairy shrine.
> With these I invoke thy gentle care,
> Queen of the earth and ambient air,
> Come with the light of thy radiant skies,
> Trace on the stream my true love's eyes,
> Show me the face in the silvery deep,
> Whose image for aye my heart may keep;

Bid the waters echoing shell,
Whisper the name thy breezes tell.
And still on the feast of Walburga's eve,
Bright young flowers to thee I'll give;
Beautiful spirit I've spoken the spell,
And offered the gift thou lovest well."

The last notes died suddenly away, and Ella, greatly agitated, threw herself into my arms. I enquired the cause of her terror, and forgetting her secrecy, she said a face had appeared to her on the stream. Just then we saw Conrad, who had followed on the same purpose I had, but had fallen and hurt his ancle, and was unable to proceed. He joined not with me when I laughed at Ella's fright, but a deeper paleness overspread his countenance. Raising his eyes to the heavens, they rested on a star beaming brightly in the blue--its mild radiance seemed to soothe him. See ye yonder, said he, how clear and unclouded the lustre of that shining orb--these words seemed irrelevant, but I knew their meaning. His knowledge of German literature had led him into the mazes of its mingled philosophy and wild romance. Astronomy and astrology were to him the same; the star to which he pointed was what he called the planet of his fate, and its brightness or obscurity were shadowed in his mind--its aspect caused him either joy or woe. The incident of Ella's fright agitated him much, for the occurrences of this real world were to him all tinged with the supernatural; but he looked again at the heavens, and the mild lustre of the star was reflected in his eyes; he leaned upon my arm, and we passed onward. I knew not then that his dark spirit felt the sunbeams which illumined mine own.

That same balmy evening I stood with Ella by the silver stream which traced its shining path around our home, watching the clear moonbeams as they flashed in the fairy foambells sparkling at our feet. There I first told my love--her hand was clasped in mine--she heard me, and raising her dewy eyes, said, "Dearest Ethel, I love you well; but not as she who weds must love you--be still to me my own dear friend and brother, and Ella will love you as she ever has. Ask not for more." She left me, and I saw a tear-drop gem the silken braid on her cheek, and thus my dream of beauty burst. My spirit's light grew dark as the treasured spell which bound me broke. Some hours passed in agony, such as none could feel but those who loved as

I did--so deep, so fondly.

As I approached my home the warm evening light was streaming from the windows, and I heard her rich voice thrilling its wild melody. Every brow smiled upon her: even Conrad's was unbent. I looked upon her, and prayed she might never know a grief like mine. The ringing music of her laugh greeted my entrance, and ere the night had passed she charmed away my woe.

While these things occurred with us, the aspect of the times without had changed. America made war with England. What were her injuries we asked not, but 'twas not likely that we, come of a race who loved so well their "fatherland and king," would join with those who had risen against theirs. As yet the crisis was not come, and in New York British power was still triumphant.

Among the many festivities given by the officers, naval and military, then in the country, was a splendid ball on board a British frigate then in the harbour. To this scene of magic beauty and delight I accompanied Ella--'twas but a few days after that unhappy first of May; but the buoyant spirits of youth are soon rekindled, and Ella yet, I thought, might love me. The scene was so new, and withal so splendid in its details, that it comes before me now fresh and undimmed. The night was one of summer's softest, earliest beauty: the moonlight slept upon the still waters, and the tall masts, with all their graceful tracery of spar and line, were bathed with rich radiance, mingled with the hundred lights of coloured lamps, suspended from festoons of flowers; low couches stood along the bulwarks of the noble ship, and the meteor flag of England, which waved so oft amid the battle and the breeze, now wafted its ruby cross o'er fair forms gliding through the dance, to the rich strains of merry music--'twas an hour that sent glad feeling to the heart. The gay dresses and noble bearing of the military officers, all glistening in scarlet and gold, contrasted well with the white robes and delicate beauty of the fair girls by their sides. But they had their rivals in the gallant givers of the fete. Many a lady's heart was lost that night. "What is it always makes a sailor so dangerous a rival?" Ella used to say, when rallied on her partiality for a "bluejacket," that she loved it because it was the colour of so many things dear to her: the sky was blue, the waves of the deep mysterious sea were blue, and the wreaths of that fairy flower, which bears the magic name forget-me-not, were of the same charmed hue. Some such reason, I suppose, it is that makes every maiden love a sailor.

While we stood gazing on the scene, enchanted and delighted, one came near and joined our group. Nobility of mind and birth was written on his brow in beauty's brightest traits. He seemed hardly nineteen, but, young as he was, many a wild breeze had parted the wavy ringlets of his hair, and the salt spray of the ocean raised a deeper hue on his cheek. His light and graceful figure was clad in the becoming costume of his rank, and on his richly braided bosom rested three half blown roses. Ella's eyes for an instant met his, they fell upon the flowers, and she dropped fainting from my arm. The mystery was soon explained. De Clairville, such was the stranger's name, had been walking on the cliffs when Ella sought the stream--he heard her voice and approached to see from whence it came--his was the face she had seen upon the waters; he heard her scream, and descended to apologise, but she was gone, and he had found and worn her rose buds--

> "Oh! there are looks and tones that dart
> An instant sunshine through the heart,
> As if the soul that instant caught
> Some treasure it through life had sought;
> As if the very lips and eyes,
> Predestined to have all our sighs,
> And never be forgot again,
> Sparkled and spoke before us then."

So sings the poet, and so seemed it with Ella and De Clairville; and when the rosy morn, tinging the eastern sky, announced to the revellers the hour of parting, that night of happiness was deemed too short.

To hasten on my story, I must merely say that they became fondly attached, and when De Clairville departed for another station, he left Ella as his betrothed bride. On love such as theirs 'twould seem to all that heaven smiled; but inscrutable to human eyes are the ways of Providence, for deadly was the blight thrown o'er them.

Meanwhile the events in which the country was engaged drew to a close. England acknowledged the independence of America, and withdrew her forces; but while she did so, offered a home and protection to those who yet wished to claim it. We were among the first to embrace the proposal: and though with sadness we left our sunny home with all its fond remembrances, yet integrity of mind was dearer still. We might not stay in the land with whose institutions we concurred not. Conrad, with his learning and talents, 'twas thought, might remain to seek the path of fame already opening to him; but what to him were the dreams of ambition, compared to the all-engrossing thought which now bound each faculty of his mind beneath its power. Ella, my mother also wished to stay, nor attempt with us the perils of our new life; for here her betrothed, when he returned, expected to meet her; but she flung her arms around my mother, saying in the language of Ruth, "thy home, dearest, shall be mine," and there shall De Clairville join us. Suffice it, then, to say, that after bidding farewell to scenes we loved, our wearisome voyage was ended, and we landed on these sterile and dreary shores. We dared not venture from the coast, and our abode was chosen in what appeared to us the best of this bleak and barren soil. 'Twas a sad change, but those were the days of strong hearts and trusting hopes.

Our settlement was formed of six or eight different households, all connected, and all from the neighbourhood of the beautiful Bowery. Each knew what the other had left, and tried to cheer each other with brighter hopes than they hardly dared to feel; but sympathy and kindness were among us.

Why need I tell you of our blighted crops and scanty harvests, and all the toil and trouble which we then endured. I must go on with what I commenced--the story of my own love. Shall I say that when Ella accompanied us I hoped De Clairville might never join us. 'Tis true, but what were my feelings to discover the love of Conrad for the gem of my heart, and that he cherished it with all the deep strength of his nature. I saw Ella's manner was not such as became a betrothed maiden, but she feared Conrad, and trembled beneath the dark glance of his eye. A feeling more of fear and pity than of love was her's; but I was fearful for the result, for I knew he was one not to be trifled with.

The last dreary days of the autumn were gathered round us--the earth was already bound in her frozen sleep, and all nature stilled in her silent trance--all, save the restless waves, dashing on the rocky shore; or the wind, which first curled their crests, and then went sweeping through the wiry foliage of the pines--when, at the close of the short twilight, we were all gathered on the highest point which overlooked the sea, earnestly gazing o'er the dim horizon, where night was coming fast. Ere the sun had set a barque had been seen, and her appearance caused unwonted excitement in our solitudes. Ships in those days were strange but welcome visitants. Not merely the necessaries of life, but kind letters and tidings from distant friends were borne by them. As the darkness increased, signal fires were raised along the beach, and ere long a gun came booming o'er the waters; soon after came the noble ship herself; her white sails gleaming through the night, and the glittering spray flashing in diamond sparkles from her prow. She came to, some distance from the shore, and, as if by magic, every sail was furled. A boat came glancing from her side; a few minutes sent it to the beach, and a gallant form sprung out upon the strand. It was De Clairville come to claim his affianced bride; and with a blushing cheek and tearful eye Ella was once more folded to his faithful heart.

A pang of jealous feeling for an instant darted through me, but Conrad's face met mine, and its dark expression drove the demon power from me. I saw the withering scowl of hate he cast upon De Clairville, and I inwardly determined to shield the noble youth from the malice of that dark one; for, bright as was to me the hope of Ella's love, I loved her too well to be ought but rejoiced in her happiness. Although it brought sorrow to myself, yet she was blessed. Mirth and joy, now for a while cheered our lonely homes; we knew we were to lose our flower; but love like theirs is a gladsome thing to look at. Many were the gifts De Clairville brought his bride from the rich shore of England. Bracelets, radiant as her own bright eyes, and pearls as pure as the neck they twined. Among other things was a fairy case of gold, in the form of a locket, which he himself wore. Ella wished to see what it contained, and laughingly he unclosed it before us: 'twas the faded rose leaves of her offerings to the love spirit on Walburga's eve. They had rested on his heart, he said, in the hours of absence; and there, in death, should they be still. Ella blushed and hid her face upon his bosom. I sighed at the memory of that day, but Conrad's gloomy frown recalled me to the present--this was their bridal eve. Our pastor was with us, and the lowly building where we worshipped was decorated with simple state for the occasion.

It stood on an eminence some distance from the other houses. That night I was awakened from sleep by a sudden light shining through the room--a wild dream' was yet before me, and a death snriek seemed ringing in my ears. I looked from the window; our little church was all in flames; 'twas built of rough logs, and was of little value, save that it was hallowed by its use. A fire had-probably been left on to prepare it for the morrow, and from this the mischief had arisen. I thought little about it, and none knew of its destruction till the morn.

The sun rose round and red, and sparkled o'er the glittering sheen of the frost king's gems, flung in wild symmetry o'er the earth, till all that before looked dark and drear was wreathed with a veil of dazzling beauty; even the blackened logs where the fire had been had their delicate tracery of pearly fringe. The guests assembled in our dwelling, and the pastor stood before the humble altar, raised for the occasion. The walls were rude, but the bride in her young beauty might have graced a palace. She leaned on Conrad's arm, according to our custom, as her oldest unmarried relative. The tables were spread with the bridal cheer, and the blazing fire crackled merrily on the wide hearth-stone. The bridegroom's presence alone was waited for. Gaily hung with flags was the ship, and cheers rung loudly from her crew as a boat left her side. It came, but bore but the officers invited to the wedding. Where was De Clairville? None knew! We had expected he passed the night on board; but there he had not been. 'Twas most strange! The day passed away, and others like it, and still he came not. He was gone for ever. Had he proved false and forsaken his love? Such was the imputation thrown on his absence by Conrad.

The sailors joined us; a band of Indian hunters led the way, and for miles around the woods were searched, but trace of human footsteps, save our own, we saw not. Long did the vessel's crew linger by the shore, hoping each day for tidings of their loved commander's fate, but of him they heard no more, and it was deemed he had met his death by drowning.

Conrad, whose morose manner suddenly disappeared for a bold and forward tone, so utterly at variance from his usual that all were surprised, still persisted in asserting that he had but proceeded along the coast, and would join his vessel as she passed onward. One of the sailors, an old and grey-haired man, who loved De Clairville as a son, indignantly denied the charge. He was incapable of such an action. "God grant," said he, "he may have been fairly dealt with." "You would not say he had been murdered," said Conrad. "No," said the old man, "I thought not of that: if he were, not a leaflet in your woods but would bear witness to the crime."

We were standing then by the ruined church--a slender beech tree grew beside it--one faded leaf yet hovered on its stem--for an instant it trembled in the blast, then fell at Conrad's feet, brushing his cheek as it passed. If the blow of a giant had struck him he could not have fallen more heavily to the ground. An inward loathing, such as may mortal man never feel to his fellow, forbade me to assist him. He had fainted; but the cold air soon revived him, and he arose, complaining of sudden illness. The sailors left us, and the ship sailed slowly from our waters, with her colours floating sadly half-mast high.

Ella thus suddenly bereaved, mourned in wild and bitter grief, but woman's pride, at times her guardian angel, at others her destroyer, took up its stronghold in her heart. The tempter Conrad awoke its tones--with specious wile he recalled De Clairville's lofty ideas of name and birth--how proudly he spoke of his lady mother and the castled state of his father's hall. Was it not likely that, at the last, this pride had rallied its strength around him, and bade him seek a nobler bride than the lowly maiden of the "Refugees?" Too readily she heard him, for love the fondest is nearest allied to hate the deepest, and De Clairville's name became a thing for scorn and hate. 'Twas vain for me to speak--what could I say? A species of fascination seemed to be obtained by Conrad o'er her--a witching spell was in his words--'twas but the power, swayed by his strong and ill-formed mind, over her weak but gentle one--which, if rightly guided, would have echoed such sweet music--and, ere the summer passed, she had forgotten her lost lover, and was to wed him.

To others there was nothing strange in this, but to me it brought a wild and dreary feeling; not that my early dreams were unchanged, for I had learned to think a love like her's, so lightly lost and won, was not the thing to be prized. Alas! I knew not the blackness of the spirit that beguiled her, and wrought such woe. Still she had done wrong--the affections of man's heart may not be idly dealt with--the woman who feigns what she feels not, has her hand on the lion's mane. Ella at one time had done this, and she reaped a dark guerdon for her falsehood. Yet in her it might have been excused, for the very weakness of her nature led her to it. Let those who are more strongly gifted beware of her fate.

The earth was in the richest flush of her green beauty. On the morn, Ella was again to be a bride--the golden light streamed through the glad blue sky, and all looked bright and fair--the remains of the church, which had long looked black and dreary, were gay with the richness of vegetation--the bracken waved its green plumes, and the tall mullen plant, with its broad white leaves, raised its pale crest above the charred walls. While the dew was shining bright I had gone forth--surprise and consternation greeted my solitary approach when I returned. Again the holy book had been opened--the priest stood ready with the bride, and tarried for the lover--they thought he was with me, but I had not seen him--daylight passed away, night came, but brought him not--the moon arose, and her shadowy light gave to familiar things of day the spectral forms of mystery.

While we sat in silence, thinking of Conrad's absence, a dog's mournful whine sounded near--it grew louder, and attracted our attention. We followed the sound--it came from the ruins of the church, and there, among the weeds and flowers lay Conrad stiff and cold--he was dead, and, oh the horrible expression of that face, the demoniac look of despair was never written in such fearful lines on human face before. All felt relief when 'twas covered from the sight. One hand had 'twined in the death grasp round the reed-like stem of the mullen plant--we unclosed it, and it sprung back, tall and straight as before; something glittered in the other--'twas the half of De Clairville's golden locket--how it came to be in his possession was strange, but we thought not of it then.

Events like these have a saddening influence on the mind, and the gloom for Conrad's sudden death hung heavy o'er us--Ella's mourning was long and deep. I was not grieved to see it, for sorrow makes the spirit wiser.

Three years passed away--little change had been among us, save that some of our aged were gone, and the young had risen around us. Once more it was the first of May--the night was dark and still, but the silvery sounds of the waging earth came like balm o'er the soul--there was a murmur in the forest, as though one heard the song of the young leaves bursting into life, and the glad gushing of the springing streams rose with them. The memory of other days was floating o'er my mind, when a soft voice broke on my reverie. Her thoughts had been with mine--"Ethel," said she, "remember you, how on such a night as this, you once sought my love. Alas! how little knew I then of my own heart--your's it should then have been--you know the shades that have passed over it. Is Ella's love a worthless gift, or will you accept it now as freely as 'tis offered. How long and sternly must we be trained e'er love's young dream can be forgotten." The events that intervened all passed away, and Ella was again the same maiden that stood with me so long ago by the stream-

let's side on Walburga's eve. My heart's long silenced music once more rung forth
its melody at her sweet words, and life again was bright with the gems of hope and
fond affection.

In places so lone as that in which we lived, the fancies of superstition have
ample scope to range. It had long been whispered through the settlement that the
spirit of Conrad appeared on the spot where he had died at certain times. When
the moon beamed, a shadowy form was seen to wave its pale arms among the ruins
of the church, which yet remained unchanged. So strongly was the story believed,
that after night-fall none dared to pass the spot alone. Ella, too, had heard it, and
trembled whilst she disbelieved its truth. Our marriage morning came, and Ella was
for the third time arrayed in her bridal dress. A wreath of pearl gleamed through her
hair, and lace and satin robed her peerless form--the tinge upon her cheek might
not have been so bright as once it was, but to me she was lovely--more of mind was
blended with the feelings of the heart, and gave a higher tone to her beauty. The
holy words were said, and my fondest hopes made truth. Is it, that because in our
most blissful hours the spirits are most ready fall, or was it the sense of coming ill
that threw its dreary shade of sadness o'er me all that day? The glorious sun sunk
brightly to his rest, but the rose cloud round his path seemed deepened to the hue
of blood. A wailing sound came o'er the waters, and a whispering, as of woe, sighed
through the leafy trees. This feeling of despondency I tried in vain to banish; as the
evening came, it grew deeper, but Ella was more joyous than ever, for a long time,
she had been. All the fairy wiles of her winning youth seemed bright as of old--glad
faces were around us, and she was the gayest of them all; when, suddenly, something from the open door met her eyes--one loud shriek broke from her, and she
rushed wildly from among us. I saw her speed madly up the hill, where stood the
church. I was hastening after, when strong arms held me back, and fingers, trembling with awe and dread, pointed to the object of their terror--there among the
ruins stood a tall and ghost-like form, whose spectral head seemed to move with a
threatening motion--for an instant I was paralysed, but Ella's white robes flashed
before me, and I broke from their grasp. Again I heard her shriek--she vanished
from me, but the phantom form still stood. I reached it, and that thing of fear was
but a gigantic weed--a tall mullen that had outgrown the others on the very spot
where we had found the body of Conrad; the waving of its flexile head and long

pale leaves, shining with moonlight, were the motions we had seen--but where was Ella? The decaying logs gave way beneath her, and she had fallen into a vault or cellar beneath the building. Meanwhile those at the house recovered their courage, and came towards us, bearing lights. We entered the vault, and, on her knees before a figure, was Ella--the form and dress were De Clairville's, such as we had seen him in last, but the face, oh! heaven, the face showed but the white bones of a skeleton. The rich brown curls still clung to the fleshless skull, and on the finger glittered the ring with which Ella was to have been wed. The half of the golden locket was clasped to his breast--the ribbon by which it hung seemed to have been torn rudely from its place, but the hand had kept its hold till the motion caused by our descent--it fell at Ella's feet, a sad memento of other days, and recalled her to sensation. Horror paled the brows of all, but to me was given a deeper woe, to think and know what Ella must have felt.

Every feeling was deepened to intensity of agony in the passing of that night--that dreary closing of my bridal day. How came the morning's light I know not, but when it did, the fresh breeze blew on my brow, and I saw the remains of De Clairville lying on the grass before me--they had borne him from below, and it showed more plainly the crime which had been among us. The deep blue of the dress was changed to a darker hue where the red life blood had flowed, and from the back was drawn the treacherous implement of death. The hearts of all readily whispered the murderer's name, and fuller proof was given in that ancient dagger that had long been an heir-loom in the family of Conrad--a relic of the old Teutonic race from whence they sprung--well was it known, and we had often wondered at its disappearance. He, Conrad, was the murderer--he had slain De Clairville, and fired the building to conceal his crime. God was the avenger of the dark deed--the mighty hand of conscience struck him in his proudest hour--the humblest things of earth, brought deathly terror to his soul. 'Twas evident the appearance of the mullen plant, which drew us to the spot, had been the cause of his death. The words of the old sailor seemed true. The lowly herb had brought the crime to light, and in the hand of heaven had punished the murderer.

We buried De Clairville beneath a mossy mound, where the lofty pine and spicy cedar waved above, and hallowed words were said o'er his rest. A blight seemed to hover o'er our lonely settlement by the deed which had been done within it. Nothing bound us to the spot; but hues of sadness rested with it, and ever would. 'Twas an unhallowed spot, and we prepared to leave it, and seek another resting place.

Our boats lay ready by the beach, and some were already embarked. I took a last look around--something white gleamed among the trees around De Clairville's grave--'twas Ella, who lay there dead. She always accused herself as the cause of De Clairville's death, and indirectly, too, she had been--but restitution now was made. We laid her by his side, and thus I lost my early, only love.

Here then was it where we chose our heritage, and here we have since remained, but everything is changed since then. Many an aged brow has passed from earth, and many a bright eye closed in death. Every trace of old is passing away, save where their shadows glide in the memory. Even the grave where Ella slept is gone from earth.

Twenty years after her death I made a pilgrimage to the place--the young sapling pines which shaded it had grown to lofty trees--human voice seemed never to have broken in tones of joy or woe the deep solitude around--the long grass waved rank and dark above the walls we had raised, and the red berries hung rich and ripe by the ruined hearthstone. Again, when another twenty years passed, I came to it once more--the weight of age had gathered o'er me, but there lay the buried sunlight of my youth, and the spirit thoughts of other days drew me to it. Again there was a change--a change which told me my own time drew near. The woods were gone long since--the reaper had passed o'er the lowly graves, and knew them not. The last record of my love and of my woe, was gone. Dwellings were raised along the lonely beach, and laden ships floated on the long silent waters. I bade the place farewell for ever, and returned to await in peace and hope my summons to the promised rest.

The old man paused--the dreams of the past had weakened him, and he retired for the night. Next morn we waited long for his presence, but he came not. We sought his chamber, and found him dead. The soul had passed away--one hand was folded on his heart, and oh! the might of earthly love. It clasped a shining braid of silken hair, and something, of which their faint perfume told to be the faded rose leaves--frail memorials of his fondly loved Ella, but lasting after the warm heart which cherished them was cold. He was gone where, if it be not in heaven "a crime to love too well," his spirit may yet meet with her's, in that holy light, whose purity of bliss may not be broken by the vain turmoil of earthly feelings. So ends the story of uncle Ethel.

       *   *   *   *   *

Well, said Grace, after we had discussed Ethel's melancholy story, although I don't believe in ghosts, I cannot do away with my faith in dreams, and last night I had a most disagreeable one, which disturbed me much. I thought I had engaged my passage, and when I unclosed my purse to pay down the money, nothing was in it but a plain gold ring and a ruby heart. My money was gone, and, oh! the grief I felt was deeper than waking language can describe. Then, Grace, said I, you must receive consolation for your disagreeable dream, in the words of your own favourite song, "Rory o'More," that dreams always go by contrary you know, and so I shall read your dream. The plain gold ring means that tie, which, like it, has no ending. The heart has, in all ages, been held symbolical of its holiest feeling, and thus unite love and marriage, and your sorrow will be turned to joy. So I prognosticate your dream to mean. And time told I had foretold aright--for soon after we had arrived in St. John's, the entrance to which, from the main river, is extremely beautiful, showing every variety of scenery, from the green meadows of rich intervale, where stand white dwellings and orchard trees, to the grey and barren rocks, with cedary plumage towering to the sky.

Grace having engaged her passage home, we were turning from the office, when a stranger bounded to us, and caught her by the hand. Grace Marley, he exclaimed--my own, my beautiful. I felt her lean heavily on my arm; she had fainted. And so deep was that trance, we fancied she was gone--but joy rarely kills, and she awoke to the passionate exclamations of her lover--for such he was, come o'er the deep sea to seek her. An explanation ensued. Their letters to each other had all miscarried. None had been received by either. (All this bitter disappointment, however, happened before the establishment of our post.) So Grace, instead of returning to Ireland, was wedded next day, her husband having brought means with him to settle in the country. The magician, Love, flung his rose-light o'er her path, and, when I saw her last, she fancied the emerald glades of Oromot, where her home now lay, almost as beautiful as those by the blue lakes of Killarney, in the land of her birth.

With the end of September commence the night frosts. The woods now lose their greenness; and the most brilliant hues of crimson, and gold, and purple, are flung in gorgeous flakes of beauty over their boughs, as though each leaf were crystal, and reflected and retained the light of some glorious sunset. In this lovely season, which is most appropriately termed the fall, we wished to **get along** with our church, and have it enclosed before the winter. This was rather an arduous undertaking in young settlement like ours; but there were those here who loved

"Old England's holy church, And loved her form of prayer right well."

And liberally they came forward to raise a temple to their faith in the wilderness. The "Society for the Propagation of the Gospel in Foreign Lands" had promised assistance; but the frame must first be erected and enclosed ere it could be claimed. In this country cash is a most scarce commodity, and many species of speculation are made with the aid of little real specie. Large sums are spoken of, but rarely appear bodily: and our church got on in the same way. The owner of the saw-mill signed twenty pounds as his subscription towards it, and paid it in boards--the carpenters who did the work received from the subscribers pork and flour for their pay--and our neighbour, the embarrassed lumber-man, who was still wooden-headed enough to like anything of a **timber spec**, got out the frame by contract, himself giving most generously five pounds worth of work towards it. And thus the church was raised, and now it stands, with white spire, pointing heavenward, above the ancient forest trees.

As winter was now approaching, how to pass its long evenings agreeably and rationally was a question which was agitated. The dwellers of America are more enlightened now than in those old times when dancing and feasting were the sole amusements, so a library was instituted and formed by the same means as the church had been--a load of potatoes, or a barrel of buckwheat, being given by each party to purchase books with. The selection of these, to suit all tastes, was a matter of some difficulty, the grave and serious declaiming against light reading, and regarding a novel as the climax of human wickedness. One old lady, who by the way was fond of reading, and had studied the ancient tale of Pamela regularly, at her leisure, for the last forty years, was the strongest against these, and, on being told that her favourite tome was no less than a novel, she consigned it to oblivion, and seemed, for a time, to have lost all faith in sublunary things. After some little trouble, however, the thing was satisfactorily arranged. Even here, to this lone nook of the western world, had reached the fame of the Caxtons of modern times. Aught that bore the name of Chambers, had a place in our collection, and the busy fingers of the little Edinburgh 'devils' have brightened the solitude of many a home on the banks of the Washedemoak.

The Indian summer, which, in November, comes like breathing space, ere the mighty power of winter sweeps o'er the earth, is beautiful, with its balmy airs and soft bright skies, yet melancholy in its loveliness as a fair face in death--'tis the last smile of summer, and when the last wreath of crimson leaves fall to earth, the erratic birds take their flight to warmer lands--the bear retires to his hollow tree--the squirrel to his winter stores--and man calls forth all his genius to make him independent of the storm king's power. In this country we have a specimen of every climate at its utmost boundary of endurance; in summer we have breathless days of burning heat shining on in shadowless splendour of sunlight; but it is in the getting up of a winter's scene that New Brunswick is perfect. True, a considerable tall sample of a snow-storm can sometimes be enjoyed in England, but nothing to compare with the free and easy sweep with which the monarch of clouds flings his boons over this portion of his dominions. After the first snow-storm the woods have a grand and beautiful appearance, festooned with their garlands of feathery pearls--the raindrops which fall with the earlier snows hang like diamond pendants, and flash in the sun, "As if gems were the fruitage of every bough."

I remember once coming from St. John's by water. The frost set in rather earlier than we expected. The farther from the sea the sooner it commences; so as we proceeded up the river our boat was stopped by the crystal barrier across the stream, not strong enough yet to admit of teaming, and we had nothing for it but a walk of seven miles through the forest,--home we must proceed, though evening was closing in and darkness would soon be around us, the heavy atmosphere told of a coming storm, and ere to-morrow our path would be blocked up. America is the land of invention; and here we were, on the dreary shore, in the dusky twilight--a situation which requires the aid of philosophy. We were something in the predicament of the Russian sailors in Spitzbergen, we wanted light to guide us on the "blaze," without which we could not keep it; but beyond the gleam of a patent congreve, our means extended not. One of our company, however, a native of the country, took the matter easy. Some birch trees were growing near, from which he stripped a portion of the silvery bark, which being rolled into torches, were ignited; each carried a store, and by their brilliant light we set out on our pilgrimage. The effect of our most original Bude on the snow-wreathed forest was magical--we seemed to traverse the palace gardens of enchantment, so strange yet splendid was the scene--the snow shining pure in the distance, and the thousand ice gems gleaming ruby red in the rays of our torches. They are wondrous to walk through, those boundless forests, when one thinks that by a slight deviation from the track the path would be lost; and, ere it could be found again, the spirit grow weary in its wanderings, and, taking its flight, leave the unshrouded brows to bleach on summer flowers or winter snows, in the path where the graceful carraboo bounds past, or the bear comes guided by the tainted breeze to where it lies.

It was on this midnight ramble that the facts of the following lines were related to me, ending not, as such tales generally do, in death, but in what perchance was worse,--civilisation lost in barbarism.

Many years ago two children, daughters of a person residing in this province, were lost in the woods. What had been their fate none knew --no trace of them could be found until, after a long period of time had elapsed, one of them was discovered among some Indians, by whom they had been taken, and with whom this one had remained, the other having joined another tribe. She appeared an Indian squaw in every respect--her complexion had been stained as dark as theirs--her costume was the same, but she had blue eyes. This excited suspicion, which proved to be correct. The story of the lost children was remembered, which event occurred thirty years before. With some difficulty she was induced to meet her mother, her only remaining parent. The tide of time swept back from the mother's mind, and she hastened to embrace the child of her memory, but, alas! the change. There existed for her no love in the bosom of the lost one. Her relatives wishing to reclaim her from her savage life, earnestly besought her to remain with them, but their ways were not as her's--she felt as a stranger with them, and rejoined the Indian band, with whom she still remains.

THE LOST CHILDREN.

At early morn a mother stood,
Her hands were raised to heaven.
And she praised Almighty God
For the blessings He had given;
But far too deep were they
Encircled in her heart,--
Too deep for human weal,
For earth and love must part.
She looked with hope too bright
On the forms that by her bent,
And loved, by far too fondly,
Those treasures God had sent.
They bound her to the earth,
With love's own golden chain,
How were its bright links severed
By the spirit's wildest pain?
She parted the rich tresses,
And kissed each snowy brow,
And where, oh! happy mother,
Was one so blest as thou?
The summer sun was shining
All cloudless o'er the lea,
When forth her children bounded,
In childhood's summer glee.
They strayed along the woody banks,
All fringed with sunny green,
Where, like a silver serpent,
The river ran between.

Their glad young voices rose,
As they thought of flower or bird,
And they sang the joyous fancies
That in each spirit stirred.
Oh! sister, see that humming bird;
Saw ye ever ought so fair?
With wings of gold and ruby,
He sparkles through the air;
Let us follow where he flies
O'er yonder hazel dell,
For oh! it must be beautiful
Where such a thing can dwell.
Yet to me it seemeth still,
That his rest must be on high;
Methinks his plumes are bathed
In the even's crimson sky:
How lovely is this earth,
Where such fair things we see,
And yet how much more glorious
The power that bids them be!
Nay, sister, let us stay
Where those water lilies float,
So spotless and so pure
Like a fairy's pearly boat.
Listen to the melody
That cometh soft and low,
As through the twining tendrils
The water glides below.
Perchance 'twas in a spot like this,
And by a stream as mild,
Where the Jewish mother laid
Her gentle Hebrew child.
Then rested they beneath the trees,

Where, through the leafy shade,
In ever-changing radiance,
The broken sun-light played;
And spoke in words, whose simple truth
Revealed the guileless soul,
Till softly o'er their senses
A quiet slumber stole.
Lo! now a form comes glancing
Along the waters blue,
And moored among the lilies
Lay an Indian's dark canoe.
The days of ancient feud were gone.
The axe was buried deep.
And stilled the red man's warfare,
In unawaking sleep.
Why stands he then so silently,
Where those fair children lie?
And say, what means the flashing
Of the Indian's eagle eye?
He thinks him of his lonely spouse,
Within her forest glade;
Around her silent dwelling
No children ever played.
No voice arose to greet him
When he at eve would come,
But sadness ever hovered
Around his dreary home.
Oh! with those lovely rose-buds
Were my lone hearth-stone blest,
My richest food should cheer them,
My softest furs should rest.
Their kindred drive us onward,
Where the setting sunbeams shine;

They claim our father's heritage,
Why may not these be mine?
He raised the sleeping children,
Oh! sad and dreary day!
And o'er the dancing waters
He bore them far away.
He wiled their hearts' young feelings
With words and actions kind,
And soon the past went fading
All dream-like from their mind.

*

*

*

*

*

Oh! brightly sped the beaming sun
Along his glorious way,
And feathery clouds of golden light
Around his parting lay.
In beauty came the holy stars,
All gleaming mid the blue,
It seemed as o'er the lovely earth
A blessed calm they threw.
A sound of grief arose
On the dewy evening air,
It bore the bitter anguish
Of a mortal's wild despair;
A wail like that which sounded
Throughout Judea's land,
When Herod's haughty minions
Obeyed his dark command.

The mourning mother wept
Because her babes were not,
Their forms were gone for ever
From each familiar spot.
Oh! had they sought the river,
And sunk beneath its wave;
Or had the dark recesses
Of the forest been their grave.
The same deep tinge of sorrow,
Each surmise ever bore;
Her gems from her were taken;
Of their fate she knew no more.
Long years of withering woe went on,
Each sadly as the last,
To other's ears the theme became
A legend of the past.
But she, oh! bright she cherished
Their memory enshrined,
With all a mother's fondness
And fadeless truth entwined.
Many a hope she treasured
In sorrow's gloom had burst,
But still her spirit knew
No grieving like the first.
Along her faded forehead
The hand of time had crost,
And every furrow told
Her mourning for the lost.
With such deep love within her,
What words the truth could give,
Howe'er she heard the tidings--
"Thy children yet they live."
But one alone was near,

And with rushing feelings wild,
The aged mother flew
To meet once more her child.
A moment passed away--
The lost one slowly came,
And stood before her there--
A tall and dark-browed dame.
Far from her swarthy forehead
Her raven hair was roll'd;
She spoke to those around her,
Her voice was stern and cold:
"Why seek ye here to bind me,
I would again be free;
They say ye are my kindred--
But what are ye to me?
My spring of youth was past
With the people of the wild:
And slumber in the green-wood
My husband and my child.
'Tis true I oft have seen ye
In the visions of the night;
But many a shadow comes
From the dreamer's land of light.
If e'er I've been among ye,
Save in my wandering thought,
The memory has passed away--
Ye long have been forgot."
And were not these hard words to come
To that fond mother's heart,
Who through such years of agony
Had kept her loving part.
Her wildest wish was granted--
Her deepest prayer was heard--

Yet it but served to show her
How deeply she had err'd.
The mysteries of God's high will
May not be understood;
And mortals may not vainly ask,
To them, what seemeth good.
With spirit wrung to earth,
In grief she bowed her head:
"Oh! better far than meet thee thus,
To mourn thee with the dead."
But, think ye, He who comforted
The widowed one of Nain--
Who bade the lonely Hagar
With hope revive again?
Think ye that mother's trusting love
Should bleed without a balm?
No! o'er the troubled spirit
There came a blessed calm.
Amid the savage relics
Around her daughter flung,
Upon her naked bosom
A crucifix there hung.
And though the simple Indian
False tenets might enthral--
Yet, 'twas the blessed symbol
Of Him who died for all.
And the mourner's heart rejoiced
For the promise seemed to say--
She shall be thine in Heaven,
When the world has passed away.
Tho' now ye meet as strangers,
Yet there ye shall be one;
And live in love for ever,

When time and earth are gone.

In the days of the early settling of the country, marriages were attended with a ceremony called stumping. This was a local way of publishing the banns, the names of the parties and the announcement of the event to take place being written on a slip of paper, and inserted on the numerous stumps bordering the corduroy road, that all who ran might read, though perchance none might scan it save some bewildered fox or wandering bear; the squire read the ceremony from the prayer-book, received his dollar, and further form for wedlock was required not. Now they order these things differently. A wedding is a regular frolic, and generally performed by a clergyman (though a few in the back settlements still adhere to the custom of their fathers), a large party being invited to solemnise the event. The last winter we were in the country we attended one some distance from home; but here, while flying along the ice paths, distance is not thought of. Nothing can be more exhilarating than sleigh-riding, the clear air bracing the nerves, and the bells ringing gladly out. These bells are worn round the horse's neck and on the harness, to give warning of the sleigh's approach, which otherwise would not be heard over the smooth road. The glassy way was crowded with skaters, gliding past with graceful ease and folded arms, "as though they trod on tented ground." We soon reached our destination, and found assembled a large and joyous party. The festival commenced in the morning, and continued late. The fare was luxuriant, and the bride, in her white dress and orange blossoms (for, be it known, such things are sometimes seen, even in this region of spruce and pine), looked as all brides do, bashful and beautiful. The "grave and pompous father," and busy-minded mother, had a look which, though concealed, told that at heart they rejoiced to see their "bairn respeckit like the lave," and "all indeed went merry as a marriage bell." We and some others left at midnight. The air was piercingly cold, and the bear skins in which we were wrapped soon had a white fringe, where fell the fast congealing breath. There was no moon, and the stars looked dim, in the fitful gleam of the streamers of the aurora borealis, which were glancing in corruscations of awful grandeur along the heavens, now throwing a blood red glare on the snow, their pale sepulchral rays of green or blue imparting a ghastly horror to the scene, or arranging themselves like the golden pillars of some mighty organ, while, ever and again, a wild unearthly sound is heard, as if swords were clashing. Those mysterious northern lights, whose appearance in superstitious times was supposed to threaten, or be the forerunner, of dire calamity; and no wonder was it, for even now, with all the light science has thrown upon such things, there is attached to them, seen as they are in this country, a feeling of dread which cannot all be dispelled.

Travelling on the ice is not altogether free from danger; and even when it is thought safe, there are places where it is dangerous to go. The best plan of avoiding these is to follow the track of those who have gone before--never, but with caution, and especially at night, striking out a new one.

One of the parties who accompanied us wished to reach the shore. There was a path which, though rather longer, would have led him safely to it, but he determined to strike across the unmarked ice, to where be wished to land. All advised him to take the longer way, but he was resolute, and turned his horse's head from us. The gallant steed bounded forward--the golden light was beaming from the sky--and we paused to watch his progress. A fearful crashing was heard--then a sharp crack, and sleigh, horse, and rider vanished from our sight. 'Twas horrible to see them thus enclosed in that cold tomb.

Assistance was speedily sought from the shore, but ere it came I heard the horrid shout of "steeds that snort in agony," while the blue sulphurous flash from above showed the man struggling helplessly among the breaking ice. Poles were placed from the solid parts to where he was, and he was rescued. He was carried to the nearest house, and with some difficulty restored to warmth. The sleighing rarely passes without many such accidents occurring, merely through want of caution.

When the balmy breezes of spring again blew ever New Brunswick, circumstances had arisen which induced me to leave it, and though I loved it not as my native land, I sighed to go, so much of kindness and good feeling had I enjoyed among its dwellers; and I stood on the vessel's deck, gazing on it till the green trees and white walls of Partridge-Island faded in the distance, and the rolling waves of the Bay of Fundy, throwing me into that least terrestrial of all maladies, the "mal du mer," rendered me insensible of all sublunary cares.

The Codes Of Hammurabi And Moses
W. W. Davies

QTY

The discovery of the Hammurabi Code is one of the greatest achievements of archaeology, and is of paramount interest, not only to the student of the Bible, but also to all those interested in ancient history...

Religion   **ISBN:** *1-59462-338-4*   **Pages:132**
MSRP $12.95

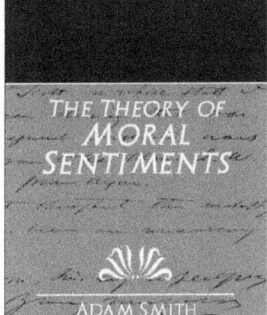

The Theory of Moral Sentiments
Adam Smith

QTY

This work from 1749. contains original theories of conscience amd moral judgment and it is the foundation for systemof morals.

Philosophy   **ISBN:** *1-59462-777-0*   **Pages:536**
MSRP $19.95

Jessica's First Prayer
Hesba Stretton

QTY

In a screened and secluded corner of one of the many railway-bridges which span the streets of London there could be seen a few years ago, from five o'clock every morning until half past eight, a tidily set-out coffee-stall, consisting of a trestle and board, upon which stood two large tin cans, with a small fire of charcoal burning under each so as to keep the coffee boiling during the early hours of the morning when the work-people were thronging into the city on their way to their daily toil...

Pages:84

Childrens   **ISBN:** *1-59462-373-2*   *MSRP $9.95*

My Life and Work
Henry Ford

QTY

Henry Ford revolutionized the world with his implementation of mass production for the Model T automobile. Gain valuable business insight into his life and work with his own auto-biography... "We have only started on our development of our country we have not as yet, with all our talk of wonderful progress, done more than scratch the surface. The progress has been wonderful enough but..."

Pages:300

Biographies/   **ISBN:** *1-59462-198-5*   *MSRP $21.95*

The Art of Cross-Examination
Francis Wellman

QTY

I presume it is the experience of every author, after his first book is published upon an important subject, to be almost overwhelmed with a wealth of ideas and illustrations which could readily have been included in his book, and which to his own mind, at least, seem to make a second edition inevitable. Such certainly was the case with me; and when the first edition had reached its sixth impression in five months, I rejoiced to learn that it seemed to my publishers that the book had met with a sufficiently favorable reception to justify a second and considerably enlarged edition. ..

Pages:412

Reference   ISBN: *1-59462-647-2*   *MSRP $19.95*

On the Duty of Civil Disobedience
Henry David Thoreau

QTY

Thoreau wrote his famous essay, On the Duty of Civil Disobedience, as a protest against an unjust but popular war and the immoral but popular institution of slave-owning. He did more than write—he declined to pay his taxes, and was hauled off to gaol in consequence. Who can say how much this refusal of his hastened the end of the war and of slavery ?

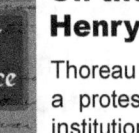

Law   ISBN: *1-59462-747-9*   **Pages:48**

MSRP $7.45

Dream Psychology Psychoanalysis for Beginners
Sigmund Freud

QTY

Sigmund Freud, born Sigismund Schlomo Freud (May 6, 1856 - September 23, 1939), was a Jewish-Austrian neurologist and psychiatrist who co-founded the psychoanalytic school of psychology. Freud is best known for his theories of the unconscious mind, especially involving the mechanism of repression; his redefinition of sexual desire as mobile and directed towards a wide variety of objects; and his therapeutic techniques, especially his understanding of transference in the therapeutic relationship and the presumed value of dreams as sources of insight into unconscious desires.

Pages:196

Psychology   ISBN: *1-59462-905-6*   *MSRP $15.45*

The Miracle of Right Thought
Orison Swett Marden

QTY

Believe with all of your heart that you will do what you were made to do. When the mind has once formed the habit of holding cheerful, happy, prosperous pictures, it will not be easy to form the opposite habit. It does not matter how improbable or how far away this realization may see, or how dark the prospects may be, if we visualize them as best we can, as vividly as possible, hold tenaciously to them and vigorously struggle to attain them, they will gradually become actualized, realized in the life. But a desire, a longing without endeavor, a yearning abandoned or held indifferently will vanish without realization.

Pages:360

Self Help   ISBN: *1-59462-644-8*   *MSRP $25.45*

QTY

The Rosicrucian Cosmo-Conception Mystic Christianity *by Max Heindel*   ISBN: *1-59462-188-8* **$38.95**
The Rosicrucian Cosmo-conception is not dogmatic, neither does it appeal to any other authority than the reason of the student. It is: not controversial, but is: sent forth in the, hope that it may help to clear...   New Age/Religion Pages 646

Abandonment To Divine Providence *by Jean-Pierre de Caussade*   ISBN: *1-59462-228-0* **$25.95**
"The Rev. Jean Pierre de Caussade was one of the most remarkable spiritual writers of the Society of Jesus in France in the 18th Century. His death took place at Toulouse in 1751. His works have gone through many editions and have been republished...   Inspirational/Religion Pages 400

Mental Chemistry *by Charles Haanel*   ISBN: *1-59462-192-6* **$23.95**
Mental Chemistry allows the change of material conditions by combining and appropriately utilizing the power of the mind. Much like applied chemistry creates something new and unique out of careful combinations of chemicals the mastery of mental chemistry...   New Age Pages 354

The Letters of Robert Browning and Elizabeth Barret Barrett 1845-1846 vol II   ISBN: *1-59462-193-4* **$35.95**
by Robert Browning and Elizabeth Barrett   Biographies Pages 596

Gleanings In Genesis (volume I) *by Arthur W. Pink*   ISBN: *1-59462-130-6* **$27.45**
Appropriately has Genesis been termed "the seed plot of the Bible" for in it we have, in germ form, almost all of the great doctrines which are afterwards fully developed in the books of Scripture which follow...   Religion/Inspirational Pages 420

The Master Key *by L. W. de Laurence*   ISBN: *1-59462-001-6* **$30.95**
In no branch of human knowledge has there been a more lively increase of the spirit of research during the past few years than in the study of Psychology, Concentration and Mental Discipline. The requests for authentic lessons in Thought Control, Mental Discipline and...   New Age/Business Pages 422

The Lesser Key Of Solomon Goetia *by L. W. de Laurence*   ISBN: *1-59462-092-X* **$9.95**
This translation of the first book of the "Lernegton" which is now for the first time made accessible to students of Talismanic Magic was done, after careful collation and edition, from numerous Ancient Manuscripts in Hebrew, Latin, and French...   New Age/Occult Pages 92

Rubaiyat Of Omar Khayyam *by Edward Fitzgerald*   ISBN:*1-59462-332-5* **$13.95**
Edward Fitzgerald, whom the world has already learned, in spite of his own efforts to remain within the shadow of anonymity, to look upon as one of the rarest poets of the century, was born at Bredfield, in Suffolk, on the 31st of March, 1809. He was the third son of John Purcell...   Music Pages 172

Ancient Law *by Henry Maine*   ISBN: *1-59462-128-4* **$29.95**
The chief object of the following pages is to indicate some of the earliest ideas of mankind, as they are reflected in Ancient Law, and to point out the relation of those ideas to modern thought.   Religion/History Pages 452

Far-Away Stories *by William J. Locke*   ISBN: *1-59462-129-2* **$19.45**
"Good wine needs no bush, but a collection of mixed vintages does. And this book is just such a collection. Some of the stories I do not want to remain buried for ever in the museum files of dead magazine-numbers an author's not unpardonable vanity..."   Fiction Pages 272

Life of David Crockett *by David Crockett*   ISBN: *1-59462-250-7* **$27.45**
"Colonel David Crockett was one of the most remarkable men of the times in which he lived. Born in humble life, but gifted with a strong will, an indomitable courage, and unremitting perseverance...   Biographies/New Age Pages 424

Lip-Reading *by Edward Nitchie*   ISBN: *1-59462-206-X* **$25.95**
Edward B. Nitchie, founder of the New York School for the Hard of Hearing, now the Nitchie School of Lip-Reading, Inc, wrote "LIP-READING Principles and Practice". The development and perfecting of this meritorious work on lip-reading was an undertaking...   How-to Pages 400

A Handbook of Suggestive Therapeutics, Applied Hypnotism, Psychic Science   ISBN: *1-59462-214-0* **$24.95**
by Henry Munro   Health/New Age/Health/Self-help Pages 376

A Doll's House: and Two Other Plays *by Henrik Ibsen*   ISBN: *1-59462-112-8* **$19.95**
Henrik Ibsen created this classic when in revolutionary 1848 Rome. Introducing some striking concepts in playwriting for the realist genre, this play has been studied the world over.   Fiction/Classics/Plays 308

The Light of Asia *by sir Edwin Arnold*   ISBN: *1-59462-204-3* **$13.95**
In this poetic masterpiece, Edwin Arnold describes the life and teachings of Buddha. The man who was to become known as Buddha to the world was born as Prince Gautama of India but he rejected the worldly riches and abandoned the reigns of power when...   Religion/History/Biographies Pages 170

The Complete Works of Guy de Maupassant *by Guy de Maupassant*   ISBN: *1-59462-157-8* **$16.95**
"For days and days, nights and nights, I had dreamed of that first kiss which was to consecrate our engagement, and I knew not on what spot I should put my lips..."   Fiction/Classics Pages 240

The Art of Cross-Examination *by Francis L. Wellman*   ISBN: *1-59462-309-0* **$26.95**
Written by a renowned trial lawyer, Wellman imparts his experience and uses case studies to explain how to use psychology to extract desired information through questioning.   How-to/Science/Reference Pages 408

Answered or Unanswered? *by Louisa Vaughan*   ISBN: *1-59462-248-5* **$10.95**
Miracles of Faith in China   Religion Pages 112

The Edinburgh Lectures on Mental Science (1909) *by Thomas*   ISBN: *1-59462-008-3* **$11.95**
This book contains the substance of a course of lectures recently given by the writer in the Queen Street Hall, Edinburgh. Its purpose is to indicate the Natural Principles governing the relation between Mental Action and Material Conditions...   New Age/Psychology Pages 148

Ayesha *by H. Rider Haggard*   ISBN: *1-59462-301-5* **$24.95**
Verily and indeed it is the unexpected that happens! Probably if there was one person upon the earth from whom the Editor of this, and of a certain previous history, did not expect to hear again...   Classics Pages 380

Ayala's Angel *by Anthony Trollope*   ISBN: *1-59462-352-X* **$29.95**
The two girls were both pretty, but Lucy who was twenty-one who supposed to be simple and comparatively unattractive, whereas Ayala was credited, as her Bombwhat romantic name might show, with poetic charm and a taste for romance. Ayala when her father died was nineteen...   Fiction Pages 484

The American Commonwealth *by James Bryce*   ISBN: *1-59462-286-8* **$34.45**
An interpretation of American democratic political theory. It examines political mechanics and society from the perspective of Scotsman James Bryce   Politics Pages 572

Stories of the Pilgrims *by Margaret P. Pumphrey*   ISBN: *1-59462-116-0* **$17.95**
This book explores pilgrims religious oppression in England as well as their escape to Holland and eventual crossing to America on the Mayflower, and their early days in New England...   History Pages 268

www.bookjungle.com *email: sales@bookjungle.com fax: 630-214-0564 mail: Book Jungle PO Box 2226 Champaign, IL 61825*

QTY

The Fasting Cure *by Sinclair Upton*   ISBN: *1-59462-222-1* **$13.95**
In the Cosmopolitan Magazine for May, 1910, and in the Contemporary Review (London) for April, 1910, I published an article dealing with my experiences in fasting, I have written a great many magazine articles, but never one which attracted so much attention... New Age/Self Help/Health Pages 164

Hebrew Astrology *by Sepharial*   ISBN: *1-59462-308-2* **$13.45**
In these days of advanced thinking it is a matter of common observation that we have left many of the old landmarks behind and that we are now pressing forward to greater heights and to a wider horizon than that which represented the mind-content of our progenitors...   Astrology Pages 144

Thought Vibration or The Law of Attraction in the Thought World   ISBN: *1-59462-127-6* **$12.95**
by William Walker Atkinson
                                                                                          Psychology/Religion Pages 144

Optimism *by Helen Keller*   ISBN: *1-59462-108-X* **$15.95**
Helen Keller was blind, deaf, and mute since 19 months old, yet famously learned how to overcome these handicaps, communicate with the world, and spread her lectures promoting optimism. An inspiring read for everyone...   Biographies/Inspirational Pages 84

Sara Crewe *by Frances Burnett*   ISBN: *1-59462-360-0* **$9.45**
In the first place, Miss Minchin lived in London. Her home was a large, dull, tall one, in a large, dull square, where all the houses were alike, and all the sparrows were alike, and where all the door-knockers made the same heavy sound...   Childrens/Classic Pages 88

The Autobiography of Benjamin Franklin *by Benjamin Franklin*   ISBN: *1-59462-135-7* **$24.95**
The Autobiography of Benjamin Franklin has probably been more extensively read than any other American historical work, and no other book of its kind has had such ups and downs of fortune. Franklin lived for many years in England, where he was agent...   Biographies/History Pages 332

Name	
Email	
Telephone	
Address	
City, State ZIP	

☐ **Credit Card**   ☐ **Check / Money Order**

Credit Card Number	
Expiration Date	
Signature	

Please Mail to: Book Jungle
PO Box 2226
Champaign, IL 61825
or Fax to: 630-214-0564

ORDERING INFORMATION

web: *www.bookjungle.com*
email: *sales@bookjungle.com*
fax: *630-214-0564*
mail: *Book Jungle PO Box 2226 Champaign, IL 61825*
or PayPal *to sales@bookjungle.com*

Please contact us for bulk discounts

DIRECT-ORDER TERMS

**20% Discount if You Order
Two or More Books**
Free Domestic Shipping!
Accepted: Master Card, Visa,
Discover, American Express

www.ingramcontent.com/pod-product-compliance
Lightning Source LLC
Chambersburg PA
CBHW082015170626
46817CB00009B/3103